Charles
SOUTH OF NO NORTH
Bukowski

BY CHARLES BUKOWSKI

The Days Run Away Like Wild Horses Over the Hills (1969)
Post Office (1971)
Mockingbird Wish Me Luck (1972)
South of No North (1973)
Burning in Water, Drowning in Flame: Selected Poems 1955–1973 (1974)
Factotum (1975)
Love Is a Dog from Hell: Poems 1974–1977 (1977)
Women (1978)
You Kissed Lilly (1978)
Play the piano drunk Like a percussion Instrument Until the fingers begin to bleed a bit (1979)
Shakespeare Never Did This (1979)
Dangling in the Tournefortia (1981)
Ham on Rye (1982)
Bring Me Your Love (1983)
Hot Water Music (1983)
There's No Business (1984)
War All the Time: Poems 1981–1984 (1984)
You Get So Alone At Times That It Just Makes Sense (1986)
The Movie: "Barfly" (1987)
The Roominghouse Madrigals: Early Selected Poems 1946–1966 (1988)
Hollywood (1989)
Septuagenarian Stew: Stories & Poems (1990)
The Last Night of the Earth Poems (1992)
Screams from the Balcony: Selected Letters 1960–1970 (Volume 1)(1993)
Pulp (1994)
Living on Luck: Selected Letters 1960s–1970s (Volume 2) (1995)
Betting on the Muse: Poems & Stories (1996)
Bone Palace Ballet: New Poems (1997)
The Captain Is Out to Lunch and the Sailors Have Taken Over the Ship (1998)
Reach for the Sun: Selected Letters 1978–1994 (Volume 3) (1999)
What Matters Most Is How Well You Walk Through the Fire: New Poems (1999)
Open All Night: New Poems (2000)
Beerspit Night and Cursing: The Correspondence of Charles Bukowski & Sheri Martinelli 1960–1967 (2001)
The Night Torn Mad with Footsteps: New Poems (2001)
Sifting Through the Madness for the Word, the Line, the Way: New Poems (2002)

Charles
Bukowski

SOUTH OF NO NORTH

Stories of the Buried Life

An Imprint of HarperCollins*Publishers*

 For information address HarperCollins Publishers Inc., 10 East 53rd Street, New York, NY 10022.

HarperCollins books may be purchased for educational, business, or sales promotional use. For information please write: Special Markets Department, HarperCollins Publishers Inc., 10 East 53rd Street, New York, NY 10022.

Grateful acknowledgment is made to the publishers of the Los Angeles *Free Press* and to Robert Head and Darlene Fife of *NOLA Express* where some of these stories originally appeared. Special thanks is also due Douglas Blazak, early publisher and supporter of Bukowski, who first published "Confessions of a Man Insane Enough to Live with Beasts" and "All the Assholes in the World and Mine" as chapbooks.

First Ecco edition published in 2003.

Library of Congress Cataloging-in-Publication Data

ISBN 0-87685-190-1
ISBN 0-87685-189-8 (PBK.)

06 07 FOLIO/RRD 10 9 8 7 6

for Ann Menebroker

TABLE OF CONTENTS

SOUTH OF NO NORTH

LONELINESS

Edna was walking down the street with her bag of groceries when she passed the automobile. There was a sign in the side window:

WOMAN WANTED.

She stopped. There was a large piece of cardboard in the window with some material pasted on it. Most of it was typewritten. Edna couldn't read it from where she stood on the sidewalk. She could only see the large letters:

WOMAN WANTED.

It was an expensive new car. Edna stepped forward on the grass to read the typewritten portion:

> Man age 49. Divorced. Wants to meet woman for marriage. Should be 35 to 44. Like television and motion pictures. Good food. I am a cost accountant, reliably employed. Money in bank. I like women to be on the fat side.

Edna was 37 and on the fat side. There was a phone number. There were also three photos of the gentleman in search of a woman. He looked quite staid in a suit and necktie. Also he looked dull and a little cruel. And made of wood, thought Edna, made of wood.

Edna walked off, smiling a bit. She also had a feeling of repulsion. By the time she reached her apartment she had forgotten about him. It was some hours later, sitting in the bathtub, that she thought about him again and this time she thought how truly lonely he must be to do such a thing:

WOMAN WANTED.

She thought of him coming home, finding the gas and phone bills in the mailbox, undressing, taking a bath, the T.V. on. Then the evening paper. Then into the kitchen to cook. Standing there in his shorts, staring down at the frying pan. Taking his food and walking to a table, eating it. Drinking his coffee. Then more T.V. And maybe a lonely can of beer before bed. There were millions of men like that all over America.

Edna got out of the tub, toweled, dressed and left her apartment. The car was still there. She took down the man's name, Joe Lighthill, and the phone number. She read the typewritten section again. "Motion pictures." What an odd term to use. People said "movies" now. *Woman Wanted*. The sign was very bold. He was original there.

When Edna got home she had three cups of coffee before dialing the number. The phone rang four times. "Hello?" he answered.

"Mr. Lighthill?"

"Yes?"

"I saw your ad. Your ad on the car."

"Oh, yes."

"My name's Edna."

"How you doing, Edna?"

"Oh, I'm all right. It's been so hot. This weather's too much."

"Yes, it makes it difficult to live."

"Well, Mr. Lighthill . . ."

"Just call me Joe."

"Well, Joe, hahaha, I feel like a fool. You know what I'm calling about?"

"You saw my sign?"

"I mean, hahaha, what's wrong with you? Can't you get a woman?"

"I guess not, Edna. Tell me, where are they?"

"Women?"

"Yes."

"Oh, everywhere, you know."

"Where? Tell me. Where?"
"Well, church, you know. There are women in church."
"I don't like church."
"Oh."
"Listen, why don't you come over, Edna?"
"You mean over there?"
"Yes. I have a nice place. We can have a drink, talk. No pressure."
"It's late."
"It's not that late. Listen you saw my sign. You must be interested."
"Well . . ."
"You're scared, that's all. You're just scared."
"No, I'm not scared."
"Then come on over, Edna."
"Well . . ."
"Come on."
"All right. I'll see you in fifteen minutes."

It was on the top floor of a modern apartment complex. Apt. 17. The swimming pool below threw back the lights. Edna knocked. The door opened and there was Mr. Lighthill. Balding in front; hawknosed with the nostril hairs sticking out; the shirt open at the neck.
"Come on in, Edna . . ."
She walked in and the door closed behind her. She had on her blue knit dress. She was stockingless, in sandals, and smoking a cigarette.
"Sit down. I'll get you a drink."
It was a nice place. Everything in blue and green and *very* clean. She heard Mr. Lighthill humming as he mixed the drinks, hmmmmmmm, hmmmmmmmm, hmmmmmmmmm . . . He seemed relaxed and it helped her.
Mr. Lighthill—Joe—came out with the drinks. He handed Edna hers and then sat in a chair across the room from her.
"Yes," he said, "it's been hot, hot as hell. I've got air-conditioning, though."
"I noticed. It's very nice."
"Drink your drink."
"Oh, yes."

Edna had a sip. It was a good drink, a bit strong but it tasted nice. She watched Joe tilt his head as he drank. He appeared to have heavy wrinkles around his neck. And his pants were much too loose. They appeared sizes too large. It gave his legs a funny look.

"That's a nice dress, Edna."

"You like it?"

"Oh yes. You're plump too. It fits you snug, real snug."

Edna didn't say anything. Neither did Joe. They just sat looking at each other and sipping their drinks.

Why doesn't he talk? thought Edna. It's up to him to talk. There *is* something wooden about him. She finished her drink.

"Let me get you another," said Joe.

"No, I really should be going."

"Oh, come on," he said, "let me get you another drink. We need something to loosen us up."

"All right, but after this one, I'm going."

Joe went into the kitchen with the glasses. He wasn't humming anymore. He came out, handed Edna her drink and sat back down in his chair across the room from her. This drink was stronger.

"You know," he said, "I do well on the sex quizzes."

Edna sipped at her drink and didn't answer.

"How do you do on the sex quizzes?" Joe asked.

"I've never taken any."

"You should, you know, so you'll find out who you are and what you are."

"Do you think those things are valid? I've seen them in the newspaper. I haven't taken them but I've seen them," said Edna.

"Of course they're valid."

"Maybe I'm no good at sex," said Edna, "maybe that's why I'm alone." She took a long drink from her glass.

"Each of us is, finally, alone," said Joe.

"What do you mean?"

"I mean, no matter how well it's going sexually or love-wise or both, the day arrives when it's over."

"That's sad," said Edna.

"Of course. So the day arrives when it's over. Either there is a split or the whole thing resolves into a truce: two people living together without feeling anything. I believe that being alone is better."

"Did you divorce your wife, Joe?"

"No, she divorced me."

"What went wrong?"

"Sexual orgies."

"Sexual orgies?"

"You know, a sexual orgy is the loneliest place in the world. Those orgies—I felt a sense of desperation—those cocks sliding in and out—excuse me . . ."

"It's all right."

"Those cocks sliding in and out, legs locked, fingers working, mouths, everybody clutching and sweating and determined to do it—somehow."

"I don't know much about those things, Joe," Edna said.

"I believe that without love, sex is nothing. Things can only be meaningful when some feeling exists between the participants."

"You mean people have to like each other?"

"It helps."

"Suppose they get tired of each other? Suppose they *have* to stay together? Economics? Children? All that?"

"Orgies won't do it."

"What does it?"

"Well, I don't know. Maybe the swap."

"The swap?"

"You know, when two couples know each other *quite* well and switch partners. Feelings, at least, have a chance. For example, say I've always liked Mike's wife. I've liked her for months. I've watched her walk across the room. I like her movements. Her movements have made me curious. I wonder, you know, what goes with those movements. I've seen her angry, I've seen her drunk, I've seen her sober. And then, the swap. You're in the bedroom with her, at last you're knowing her. There's a chance for something real. Of course, Mike has your wife in the other room. Good luck, Mike, you think, and I hope you're as good a lover as I am."

"And it works all right?"

"Well, I dunno . . . Swaps can cause difficulties . . . afterwards. It all has to be talked out . . . very well talked out ahead of time. And then maybe people don't know enough, no matter how much they talk . . ."

"Do you know enough, Joe?"

"Well, these swaps . . . I think it might be good for some . . . maybe good for many. I guess it wouldn't work for me. I'm too much of a prude."

Joe finished his drink. Edna set the remainder of hers down and stood up.

"Listen Joe, I have to be going . . ."

Joe walked across the room toward her. He looked like an elephant in those pants. She saw his big ears. Then he grabbed her and was kissing her. His bad breath came through all the drinks. He had a very sour smell. Part of his mouth was not making contact. He was strong but his strength was not pure, it begged. She pulled her head away and still he held her.

WOMAN WANTED.

"Joe, let me go! You're moving too *fast*, Joe! Let go!"

"Why did you come here, bitch?"

He tried to kiss her again and succeeded. It was horrible. Edna brought her knee up. She got him good. He grabbed and fell to the rug.

."God, god . . . why'd you have to do that? You tried to kill me . . ."

He rolled on the floor.

His behind, she thought, he had such an *ugly* behind.

She left him rolling on the rug and ran down the stairway. The air was clean outside. She heard people talking, she heard their T.V. sets. It wasn't a long walk to her apartment. She felt the need of another bath, got out of her blue knit dress and scrubbed herself. Then she got out of the tub, toweled herself dry and set her hair in pink curlers. She decided not to see him again.

BOP BOP AGAINST THAT CURTAIN

We talked about women, peeked up their legs as they got out of cars, and we looked into windows at night hoping to see somebody fucking but we never saw anybody. One time we did watch a couple in bed and the guy was mauling his woman and we thought now we're going to see it, but she said, "No, I don't want to do it tonight!" Then she turned her back on him. He lit a cigarette and we went in search of a new window.

"Son of a bitch, no woman of mine would turn away from me!"

"Me neither. What kind of a man was that?"

There were three of us, me, Baldy, and Jimmy. Our big day was Sunday. On Sunday we met at Baldy's house and took the streetcar down to Main Street. Carfare was seven cents.

There were two burlesque houses in those days, the Follies and the Burbank. We were in love with the strippers at the Burbank and the jokes were a little better so we went to the Burbank. We had tried the dirty movie house but the pictures weren't really dirty and the plots were all the same. A couple of guys would get some little innocent girl drunk and before she got over her hangover she'd find herself in a house of prostitution with a line of sailors and hunchbacks beating on her door. Besides in those places the bums slept night and day, pissed on the floor, drank wine, and rolled each other. The stink of piss and wine and murder was unbearable. We went to the Burbank.

"You boys going to a burlesque today?" Baldy's grampa would ask.

"Hell no, sir, we've got things to do."

We went. We went each Sunday. We went early in the morning, long before the show and we walked up and down Main Street looking into the empty bars where the B-girls sat in the doorways with their skirts up, kicking their ankles in the sunlight that drifted into the dark bar. The girls looked good. But we knew. We had heard. A guy went in for a drink and they charged his ass off, both for his drink and the girl's. But the girl's drink would be watered. You'd get a feel or two and that was it. If you showed any money the barkeep would see it and along would come the mickey and you were out over the bar and your money was gone. We knew.

After our walk along Main Street we'd go into the hotdog place and get our eight cent hotdog and our big nickel mug of rootbeer. We were lifting weights and our muscles bulged and we wore our sleeves rolled high and we each had a pack of cigarettes in our breast pocket. We even had tried a Charles Atlas course, Dynamic Tension, but lifting weights seemed the more rugged and obvious way.

While we ate our hotdog and drank our huge mug of rootbeer we played the pinball machine, a penny a game. We got to know that pinball machine very well. When you made a perfect score you got a free game. We had to make perfect scores, we didn't have that kind of money.

Franky Roosevelt was in, things were getting better but it was still the depression and none of our fathers were working. Where we got our small amount of pocket money was a mystery except that we did have a sharp eye for anything that was not cemented to the ground. We didn't steal, we shared. And we invented. Having little or no money we invented little games to pass the time—one of them being to walk to the beach and back.

This was usually done on a summer day and our parents never complained when we arrived home too late for dinner. Nor did they care about the high glistening blisters on the bottoms of our feet. It was when they saw how we had worn out our heels and the soles of our shoes that we began to hear it. We were sent to the five and dime store where heels and soles and glue were at the ready and at a reasonable price.

The situation was the same when we played tackle football in the streets. There weren't any public funds for playgrounds. We were so tough we played tackle football in the streets all through football season, through basketball and baseball seasons and on through the next football season. When you get tackled on asphalt, things happen. Skin rips, bones bruise, there's blood, but you get up like nothing was wrong.

Our parents never minded the scabs and the blood and the bruises; the terrible and unforgivable sin was to rip a *hole* in one of the knees of your pants. Because there were only two pairs of pants to each boy: his everyday pants and his Sunday pants, and you could never rip a hole in the knee of one of your two pairs of pants because that showed that you were poor and an asshole and that your parents were poor and assholes too. So you learned to tackle a guy without falling on *either* knee. And the guy being tackled learned how to be tackled without falling on either knee.

When we had fights we'd fight for hours and our parents wouldn't save us. I guess it was because we pretended to be so tough and never asked for mercy, they were waiting for us to ask for mercy. But we hated our parents so we couldn't and because we hated them they hated us, and they'd walk out on their porches and glance casually over at us in the midst of a terrible endless fight. They'd just yawn and pick up a throw-away advertisement and walk back inside.

I fought a guy who later ended up very high in the United States Navy. I fought him one day from 8:30 in the morning until after sundown. Nobody stopped us although we were in plain sight of his front lawn, under two huge pepper trees with the sparrows shitting on us all day.

It was a grim fight, it was to the finish. He was bigger, a little older and heavier, but I was crazier. We quit by common consent—I don't know how this works, you have to experience it to understand it, but after two people beat on each other eight or nine hours a strange kind of brotherhood emerges.

The next day my body was entirely blue. I couldn't speak out of my lips or move any part of myself without pain. I was on the bed getting ready to die and my mother came in with the shirt I'd worn during the fight. She held it in front of my face over the bed and she said, "Look, you got bloodspots on this shirt! Bloodspots!"

"Sorry!"

"I'll never get them out! NEVER!!"

"They're *his* bloodspots."

"It doesn't matter! It's blood! It doesn't come out!"

Sundays were our day, our quiet, easy day. We went to the Burbank. There was always a bad movie first. A very old movie, and you looked and waited. You were thinking of the girls. The three or four guys in the orchestra pit, they played loud, maybe they didn't play too good but they played loud, and those strippers finally came out and grabbed the curtain, the edge of the curtain, and they grabbed that curtain like it was a man and shook their bodies and went bop bop bop against that curtain. Then they swung out and started to strip. If you had enough money there was even a bag of popcorn; if you didn't to hell with it.

Before the next act there was an intermission. A little man got up and said, "Ladies and gentlemen, if you will let me have your kind attention . . ." He was selling peep-rings. In the glass of each ring, if you held it to the light there was a most wonderful picture. This was promised you! Each ring was only 50 cents, a lifetime possession for just 50 cents, made available only to the patrons of the Burbank and not sold anywhere else. "Just hold it up to the light and you will see! And, thank you, ladies and gentlemen, for your kind attention. Now the ushers will pass down the aisles among you."

Two ragass bums would proceed down the aisles smelling of muscatel, each carrying a bag of peep-rings. I never saw anybody purchase one of the rings. I imagine, though, if you had held one up to the light the picture in the glass would have been a naked woman.

The band began again and the curtains opened and there was the chorus line, most of them former strippers gone old, heavy with mascara and rouge and lipstick, false eyelashes. They did their damndest to stay with the music but they were always a little behind. But they carried on; I thought they were very brave.

Then came the male singer. It was very difficult to like the male singer. He sang too loud about love gone wrong. He didn't know how to sing and when he finished he spread his arms, and bowed his head to the tiniest ripple of applause.

Then came the comedian. Oh, he was good! He came out in an old brown overcoat, hat pulled down over his eyes, slouching and walking like a bum, a bum with nothing to do and no place to go. A girl would walk by on the stage and his eyes would follow her. Then he'd turn to the audience and say, out of his toothless mouth, "Well, I'll be god damned!"

Another girl would walk out on the stage and he'd walk up to her, put his face close to hers and say, "I'm an old man, I'm past but when the bed breaks down I finish on the floor." That did it. How we laughed! The young guys and the old guys, how we laughed. And there was the suitcase routine. He's trying to help some girl pack her suitcase. The clothes keep popping out.

"I can't get it in!"

"Here let me help you!"

"It popped out again!"

"Wait! I'll stand on it!"

"What? Oh *no*, you're not going to *stand* on it!"

They went on and on with the suitcase routine. Oh, he was funny!

Finally the first three or four strippers came out again. We each had our favorite stripper and we each were in love. Baldy had chosen a thin French girl with asthma and dark pouches under her eyes. Jimmy liked the Tiger Woman (properly The Tigress). I pointed out to Jimmy the Tiger Woman definitely had one breast larger than the other. Mine was Rosalie.

Rosalie had a large ass and she shook it and shook it and sang funny little songs, and as she walked about stripping she talked to herself and giggled. She was the only one who really enjoyed her work. I was in love with Rosalie. I often thought of writing her and telling her how great she was but somehow I never got around to it.

One afternoon we were waiting for the streetcar after the show and there was the Tiger Woman waiting for the streetcar too. She was dressed in a tight-fitting green dress and we stood there looking at her.

"It's your girl, Jimmy, it's the Tiger Woman."

"Boy, she's got it! Look at her!"

"I'm going to talk to her," said Baldy.

"It's Jimmy's girl."

"I don't want to talk to her," said Jimmy.

"I'm going to talk to her," said Baldy. He put a cigarette in his mouth, lit it, and walked up to her.

"Hi ya, baby!" he grinned at her.

The Tiger Woman didn't answer. She just stared straight ahead waiting for the streetcar.

"I know who you are. I saw you strip today. You've got it, baby, you've really got it!"

The Tiger Woman didn't answer.

"You really shake it, my god, you really shake it!"

The Tiger Woman stared straight ahead. Baldy stood there grinning like an idiot at her. "I'd like to put it to you. I'd like to fuck you, baby!"

We walked up and pulled Baldy away. We walked him down the street. "You asshole, you have no right to talk to her that way!"

"Well, she gets up and shakes it, she gets up in front of men and shakes it!"

"She's just trying to make a living."

"She's hot, she's red hot, she wants it!"

"You're crazy."

We walked him down the street.

Not long after that I began to lose interest in those Sundays on Main Street. I suppose the Follies and the Burbank are still there. Of course, the Tiger Woman and the stripper with asthma, and Rosalie, my Rosalie are long gone. Probably dead. Rosalie's big shaking ass is probably dead. And when I'm in my neighborhood, I drive past the house I used to live in and there are strangers living there. Those Sundays were good, though, most of those Sundays were good, a tiny light in the dark depression days when our fathers walked the front porches, jobless and impotent and glanced at us beating the shit out of each other, then went inside and stared at the walls, afraid to play the radio because of the electric bill.

YOU AND YOUR BEER AND HOW GREAT YOU ARE

Jack came through the door and found the pack of cigarettes on the mantle. Ann was on the couch reading a copy of *Cosmopolitan.* Jack lit up, sat down in a chair. It was ten minutes to midnight.

"Charley told you not to smoke," said Ann, looking up from the magazine.

"I deserve it. It was a rough one tonight."

"Did you win?"

"Split decision but I got it. Benson was a tough boy, lots of guts. Charley says Parvinelli is next. We get over Parvinelli, we get the champ."

Jack got up, went to the kitchen, came back with a bottle of beer.

"Charley told me to keep you off the beer," Ann put the magazine down.

" 'Charley told me, Charley told me' . . . I'm tired of that. I won my fight. I won 16 straight, I got a right to a beer and a cigarette."

"You're supposed to stay in shape."

"It doesn't matter. I can whip any of them."

"You're so great, I keep hearing it when you get drunk, you're so great. I get sick of it."

"I am great. 16 straight, 15 k.o.'s. Who's better?"

Ann didn't answer. Jack took his bottle of beer and his cigarette into the bathroom.

"You didn't even kiss me hello. The first thing you did was go to your bottle of beer. You're so great, all right. You're a great beer-drinker."

Jack didn't answer. Five minutes later he stood in the bathroom door, his pants and shorts down around his shoes.

"Jesus Christ, Ann, can't you even keep a roll of toilet paper in here?"

"Sorry."

She went to the closet and got him the roll. Jack finished his business and walked out. Then he finished his beer and got another one. "Here you are living with the best light-heavy in the world and all you do is complain. Lots of girls would love to have me but all you do is sit around and bitch."

"I know you're good, Jack, maybe the best, but you don't know how *boring* it is to sit around and listen to you say over and over again how great you are."

"Oh, you're bored with it, are you?"

"Yes, god damn it, you and your beer and how great you are."

"Name a better light-heavy. You don't even come to my fights."

"There are *other* things besides fighting, Jack."

"What? Like laying around on your ass and reading *Cosmopolitan?*"

"I like to improve my mind."

"You ought to. There's a lot of work to be done there."

"I tell you there are other things besides fighting."

"What? Name them."

"Well, art, music, painting, things like that."

"Are you any good at them?"

"No, but I appreciate them."

"Shit, I'd rather be best at what I'm doing."

"Good, better, best . . . God, can't you appreciate people for what they are?"

"For what they *are?* What *are* most of them? Snails, bloodsuckers, dandies, finks, pimps, servants . . ."

"You're always looking down on everybody. None of your friends are good enough. You're so damned great!"

"That's right, baby."

Jack walked into the kitchen and came out with another beer.

"You and your god damned beer!"

"It's my right. They sell it. I buy it."

"Charley said . . ."

"Fuck Charley!"

"You're so god damned great!"

"That's right. At least Pattie knew it. She admitted it. She was proud of it. She knew it took something. All you do is bitch."

"Well, why don't you go back to Pattie? What are you doing with me?"

"That's just what I'm thinking."

"Well, we're not married, I can leave any time."

"That's one break we've got. Shit, I come in here dead-ass tired after a tough ten rounder and you're not even glad I took it. All you do is complain about me."

"Listen, Jack, there are other things besides fighting. When I met you, I admired you for what you were."

"I was a fighter. There *aren't* any other things besides fighting.

That's what I am—a fighter. That's my life, and I'm good at it. The best. I notice you always go for those second raters . . . like Toby Jorgenson."

"Toby's very funny. He's got a sense of humor, a real sense of humor. I like Toby."

"His record is 9, 5, and one. I can take him when I'm dead drunk."

"And god knows you're dead drunk often enough. How do you think I feel at parties when you're laying on the floor passed out, or lolling around the room telling everybody, 'I'M GREAT, I'M GREAT, I'M GREAT!' Don't you think that makes me feel like an ass?"

"Maybe you are an ass. If you like Toby so much, why don't you go with him?"

"Oh, I just said I liked him, I thought he was *funny*, that doesn't mean I want to go to bed with him."

"Well, you go to bed with me and you say I'm boring. I don't know what the hell you want."

Ann didn't answer. Jack got up, walked over to the couch, lifted Ann's head and kissed her, walked back and sat down again.

"Listen, let me tell you about this fight with Benson. Even you would have been proud of me. He decks me in the first round, a sneak right. I get up and hold him off the rest of the round. He plants me again in the second. I barely get up at 8. I hold him off again. The next few rounds I spend getting my legs back. I take the 6th, 7th, 8th, deck him once in the 9th and twice in the 10th. I don't call that a split. They called it a split. Well, it's 45 grand, you get that, kid? 45 grand. I'm great, you can't deny I'm great, can you?"

Ann didn't answer.

"Come on, tell me I'm great."

"All right, you're great."

"Well, that's more like it." Jack walked over and kissed her again. "I feel so good. Boxing is a work of art, it really is. It takes guts to be a great artist and it takes guts to be a great fighter."

"All right, Jack."

" 'All right, Jack,' is that all you can say? Pattie used to be happy when I won. We were both happy all night. Can't you share it when I do something good? Hell, are you in love with me or are you in love with the losers, the half-asses? I think you'd be happier if I came in here a loser."

"I want you to win, Jack, it's only that you put so much emphasis on what you do . . ."

"Hell, it's my living, it's my life. I'm proud of being best. It's like flying, it's like flying off into the sky and whipping the sun."

"What are you going to do when you can't fight anymore?"

"Hell, we'll have enough money to do whatever we want."

"Except get along, maybe."

"Maybe I can learn to read *Cosmopolitan*, improve my mind."

"Well, there's room for improvement."

"Fuck you."

"What?"

"Fuck you."

"Well, that's something you haven't done in a while."

"Some guys like to fuck bitching women, I don't."

"I suppose Pattie didn't bitch?"

"All women bitch, you're the champ."

"Well, why don't you go back to Pattie?"

"You're here now. I can only house one whore at a time."

"Whore?"

"Whore."

Ann got up and went to the closet, got out her suitcase and began putting her clothes in there. Jack went to the kitchen and got another bottle of beer. Ann was crying and angry. Jack sat down with his beer and took a good drain. He needed a whiskey, he needed a bottle of whiskey. And a good cigar.

"I can come pick up the rest of my stuff when you're not around."

"Don't bother. I'll have it sent to you."

She stopped at the doorway.

"Well, I guess this is it," she said.

"I suppose it is," Jack answered.

She closed the door and was gone. Standard procedure. Jack finished the beer and went over to the telephone. He dialed Pattie's number. She answered.

"Pattie?"

"Oh, Jack, how are you?"

"I won the big one tonight. A split. All I got to do is get over Parvinelli and I got the champ."

"You'll whip both of them, Jack. I know you can do it."

"What are you doing tonight, Pattie?"

"It's 1:00 a.m. Jack. Have you been drinking?"

"A few. I'm celebrating."

"How about Ann?"

"We split. I only play one woman at a time, you know that Pattie."

"Jack . . ."

"What?"

"I'm with a guy."

"A guy?"

"Toby Jorgenson. He's in the bedroom . . ."

"Oh, I'm sorry."

"I'm sorry, too, Jack, I loved you . . . maybe I still do."

"Oh, shit, you women really throw that word around . . ."

"I'm sorry, Jack."

"It's o.k." He hung up. Then he went to the closet for his coat. He put it on, finished the beer, went down the elevator to his car. He drove straight up Normandie at 65 m.p.h., pulled into the liquor store on Hollywood Boulevard. He got out and walked in. He got a six-pack of Michelob, a pack of Alka-Seltzers. Then at the counter he asked the clerk for a fifth of Jack Daniels. While the clerk was tabbing them up a drunk walked up with two six-packs of Coors.

"Hey, man!" he said to Jack, "ain't you Jack Backenweld, the fighter?"

"I am," answered Jack.

"Man, I saw that fight tonight, Jack, you're all guts. You're really great!"

"Thanks, man," he told the drunk, and then he took his sack of goods and walked to his car. He sat there, took the cap off the Daniels and had a good slug. Then he backed out, ran west down Hollywood, took a left at Normandie and noticed a well-built teenage girl staggering down the street. He stopped his car, lifted the fifth out of the bag and showed it to her.

"Want a ride?"

Jack was surprised when she got in. "I'll help you drink that, mister, but no fringe benefits."

"Hell, no" said Jack.

He drove down Normandie at 35 m.p.h., a self-respecting citizen and third ranked light-heavy in the world. For a moment he felt like telling her who she was riding with but he changed his mind and reached over and squeezed one of her knees.

"You got a cigarette, mister?" she asked.

He flicked one out with his hand, pushed in the dash lighter. It jumped out and he lit her up.

NO WAY TO PARADISE

I was sitting in a bar on Western Ave. It was around midnight and I was in my usual confused state. I mean, you know, nothing works right: the women, the jobs, the no jobs, the weather, the dogs. Finally you just sit in a kind of stricken state and wait like you're on the bus stop bench waiting for death.

Well, I was sitting there and here comes this one with long dark hair, a good body, sad brown eyes. I didn't turn on for her. I ignored her even though she had taken the stool next to mine when there were a dozen other empty seats. In fact, we were the only ones in the bar except for the bartender. She ordered a dry wine. Then she asked me what I was drinking.

"Scotch and water."

"Give him a scotch and water," she told the barkeep.

Well, that was unusual.

She opened her purse, removed a small wire cage and took some little people out and sat them on the bar. They were all around three inches tall and they were alive and properly dressed. There were four of them, two men and two women.

"They make these now," she said, "they're very expensive. They cost around $2,000 apiece when I got them. They go for around $2,400 now. I don't know the manufacturing process but it's probably against the law."

The little people were walking around on the top of the bar. Suddenly one of the little guys slapped one of the little women across the face.

"You bitch," he said, "I've had it with you!"

"No, George, you can't," she cried, "I love you! I'll kill myself! I've got to have you!"

"I don't care," said the little guy, and he took out a tiny cigarette and lit it. "I've got a right to live."

"If you don't want her," said the other little guy, "I'll take her. I love her."

"But I don't want you, Marty. I'm in love with George."

"But he's a bastard, Anna, a real bastard!"

"I know, but I love him anyhow."

The little bastard then walked over and kissed the other little woman.

"I've got a triangle going," said the lady who had bought me the drink. "That's Marty and George and Anna and Ruthie. George goes down, he goes down good. Marty's kind of square."

"Isn't it sad to watch all that? Er, what's your name?"

"Dawn. It's a terrible name. But that's what mothers do to their children sometimes."

"I'm Hank. But isn't it sad . . ."

"No, it isn't sad to watch it. I haven't had much luck with my own loves, terrible luck really . . ."

"We all have terrible luck."

"I suppose. Anyhow, I bought these little people and now I watch them, and it's like having it and not having any of the problems. But I get awfully hot when they start making love. That's when it gets difficult."

"Are they sexy?"

"Very, very sexy. My god, it makes me hot!"

"Why don't you make them do it? I mean, right now. We'll watch them together."

"Oh, you can't make them do it. They've got to do it on their own."

"How often do they do it?"

"Oh, they're pretty good. They go four or five times a week."

They were walking around on the bar. "Listen," said Marty, "give me a chance. Just give me a chance, Anna."

"No," said Anna, "my love belongs to George. There's no other way it can be."

George was kissing Ruthie, feeling her breasts. Ruthie was getting hot.

"Ruthie's getting hot," I told Dawn.

"She is. She really is."

I was getting hot too. I grabbed Dawn and kissed her.

"Listen," she said, "I don't like them to make love in public. I'll take them home and have them do it."

"But then I can't watch."

"Well, you'll just have to come with me."

"All right," I said, "let's go."

I finished my drink and we walked out together. She carried the little people in the small wire cage. We got into her car and put the people in between us on the front seat. I looked at Dawn. She was really young and beautiful. She seemed to have good insides too. How could she have gone wrong with her men? There were so many ways those things could miss. The four little people had cost her $8,000. Just *that* to get away from relationships and *not* to get away from relationships.

Her house was near the hills, a pleasant looking place. We got out and walked up to the door. I held the little people in the cage while Dawn opened the door.

"I heard Randy Newman last week at The Troubador. Isn't he great?" she asked.

"Yes, he is."

We walked into the front room and Dawn took the little people out and placed them on the coffeetable. Then she walked into the kitchen and opened the refrigerator and got out a bottle of wine. She brought in two glasses.

"Pardon me," she said, "but you seem a little bit crazy. What do you do?"

"I'm a writer."

"Are you going to write about this?"

"They'll never believe it, but I'll write it."

"Look," said Dawn, "George has got Ruthie's panties off. He's fingering her. Ice?"

"Yes, he is. No, no ice. Straight's fine."

"I don't know," said Dawn, "it really gets me hot to watch them. Maybe it's because they're so small. It really heats me up."

"I know what you mean."

"Look, George is going down on her now."

"He is, isn't he?"

"Look at them!"

"God o mighty!"

I grabbed Dawn. We stood there kissing. As we did her eyes went from mine to them and then back to mine again.

Little Marty and little Anna were watching too.

"Look," said Marty, "they're going to make it. We might as well make it. Even the big folks are going to make it. Look at them!"

"Did you hear that?" I asked Dawn. "They said we're going to make it. Is that true?"

"I hope it's true," said Dawn.

I got her over to the couch and worked her dress up around her hips. I kissed her along the throat. "I love you," I said.

"Do you? Do you?"

"Yes, somehow, yes . . ."

"All right," said little Anna to little Marty, "we might as well do it too, even though I don't love you."

They embraced in the middle of the coffeetable. I had worked Dawn's panties off. Dawn groaned. Little Ruthie groaned. Marty closed in on Anna. It was happening everywhere. I got the idea that everybody in the world was doing it. Then I forgot about the rest of the world. We somehow walked into the bedroom. Then I got into Dawn for the long slow ride. . . .

When she came out of the bathroom I was reading a dull dull story in *Playboy*.

"It was so good," she said.

"My pleasure," I answered.

She got back into bed with me. I put the magazine down.

"Do you think we can make it together?" she asked.

"What do you mean?"

"I mean, do you think we can make it together for any length of time?"

"I don't know. Things happen. The beginning is always easiest."

Then there was a scream from the front room. "Oh-oh," said Dawn. She leaped up and ran out of the room. I followed. When I got there she was holding George in her hands.

"Oh, my god!"

"What happened?"

"Anna did it to him!"

"Did what?"

"She cut off his balls! George is a eunuch!"

"Wow!"

"Get me some toilet paper, quickly! He might bleed to death!"

"That son of a bitch," said little Anna from the coffeetable, "if

I can't have George, nobody can have him!"

"Now both of you belong to me!" said Marty.

"No, you've got to choose between us," said Anna.

"Which one of us is it?" asked Ruthie.

"I love you both," said Marty.

"He's stopped bleeding," said Dawn. "He's out cold." She wrapped George in a handkerchief and put him on the mantle.

"I mean," Dawn said to me, "if you don't think we can make it, I don't want to go into it anymore."

"I think I love you, Dawn."

"Look," she said, "Marty's embracing Ruthie!"

"Are they going to make it?"

"I don't know. They seem excited."

Dawn picked Anna up and put her in the wire cage.

"Let me out of here! I'll kill both of them! Let me out of here!"

George moaned from inside his handkerchief upon the mantle. Marty had Ruthie's panties off. I pulled Dawn to me. She was beautiful and young and had insides. I could be in love again. It was possible. We kissed. I fell down inside her eyes. Then I got up and began running. I knew where I was. A cockroach and an eagle made love. Time was a fool with a banjo. I kept running. Her long hair fell across my face.

"I'll kill everybody!" screamed little Anna. She rattled about in her wire cage at 3 a.m. in the morning.

POLITICS

At L.A. City College just before World War II, I posed as a Nazi. I hardly knew Hitler from Hercules and cared less. It was just that sitting in class and hearing all the patriots preach how we should go over and do the beast in, I grew bored. I decided to become the opposition. I didn't even bother to read up on Adolf, I simply spouted anything that I felt was evil or maniacal.

However, I really didn't have any political beliefs. It was a way of floating free.

You know, sometimes if a man doesn't believe in what he is doing he can do a much more interesting job because he isn't emotionally caught up in his Cause. It wasn't long before all the tall blond boys had formed The Abraham Lincoln Brigade—to hold off the hordes of fascism in Spain. And then had their asses shot off by trained troops. Some of them did it for adventure and a trip to Spain but they still got their asses shot off. I liked my ass. There really wasn't much I liked about myself but I did like my ass and my pecker.

I leaped up in class and shouted anything that came to my mind. Usually it had something to do with the Superior Race, which I thought was rather humorous. I didn't lay it directly onto the Blacks and the Jews because I saw that they were as poor and confused as I was. But I did get off some wild speeches in and out of class, and the bottle of wine I kept in my locker helped me along. I was surprised that so many people listened to me and how few, if any, ever questioned my statements. I just ran off at the mouth and was delighted at how entertaining L.A. City College could be.

"Are you going to run for student body president, Chinaski?"

"Shit, no."

I didn't want to do anything. I didn't even went to go to gym. In fact, the last thing I wanted to do was to go to gym and sweat and wear a jockstrap and compare pecker-lengths. I knew I had a medium-sized pecker. I didn't have to take gym to establish that.

We were lucky. The college decided to charge a two dollar enrollment fee. We decided—a few of us decided, anyhow—that *that* was unconstitutional, so we refused. We struck against it. The college allowed us to attend classes but took away some of our privileges, one of them being gym.

When time arrived for gym class, we stood in civilian clothing. The coach was given orders to march us up and down the field in close formation. That was their revenge. Beautiful. I didn't have to run around the track with my ass sweating or try to throw a demented basketball through a demented hoop.

We marched back and forth, young, full of piss, full of madness, oversexed, cuntless, on the edge of war. The less you believed in life the less you had to lose. I didn't have very much to lose, me and my medium-sized cock.

We marched around and made up dirty songs, and the good American boys on the football team threatened to whip our asses but somehow never got around to it. Probably because we were bigger and meaner. To me, it was wonderful, pretending to be a Nazi, and then turning around and proclaiming that my constitutional rights were being violated.

I did sometimes get emotional. I remember one time in class, after a little too much wine, with a tear in each eye, I said, "I promise you, this will hardly be the last war. As soon as one enemy is eliminated somehow another is found. It's endless and meaningless. There's no such thing as a good war or a bad war."

Another time there was a communist speaking from a platform on a vacant lot south of the campus. He was a very earnest boy with rimless glasses, pimples, wearing a black sweater with holes in the elbows. I stood listening and had some of my disciples with me. One of them was a White Russian, Zircoff, his father or his grandfather had been killed by the Reds in the Russian revolution. He showed me a sack of rotten tomatoes. "When you give the word," he told me, "we'll begin throwing them."

It occurred to me suddenly that my disciples hadn't been listening to the speaker, or even if they had been, nothing he had said would matter. Their minds were made up. Most of the world was like that. Having a medium-sized cock suddenly didn't seem the world's worst sin.

"Zircoff," I said, "put the tomatoes away."

"Piss," he said, "I wish they were hand grenades."

I lost control of my disciples that day, and walked away as they started hurling their rotten tomatoes.

I was informed that a new Vanguard Party was to be formed. I was given an address in Glendale and I went there that night. We sat in the basement of a large home with our wine bottles and our various-sized cocks.

There was a platform and desk with a large American flag spread across the back wall. A healthy looking American boy walked out on the platform and suggested that we begin by saluting the flag, pledging allegiance to it.

I always disliked pledging allegiance to the flag. It was so tedious and sillyass. I always felt more like pledging allegiance to myself, but there we were and we stood up and ran through it. Then, afterwards, the little pause, and everybody sitting down feeling as if they had been slightly molested.

The healthy American began talking. I recognized him as a fat boy who sat in the front row of the playwriting class. I never trusted those types. Sucks. Strictly sucks. He began: "The Communist menace *must* be stopped. We are gathered here to take steps to do so. We will take lawful steps and, perhaps, unlawful steps to do this . . ."

I don't remember much of the rest. I didn't care about the Communist menace or the Nazi menace. I wanted to get drunk, I wanted to fuck, I wanted a good meal, I wanted to sing over a glass of beer in a dirty bar and smoke a cigar. I wasn't aware. I was a dupe, a tool.

Afterwards, Zircoff and myself and one ex-disciple went down to Westlake Park and we rented a boat and tried to catch a duck for dinner. We managed to get very drunk and didn't catch a duck and found we didn't have enough money between us to pay the boat rental fee.

We floated around the shallow lake and played Russian Roulette with Zircoff's gun and we all lucked through. Then Zircoff stood up in the moonlight drunk and shot the hell out of the bottom of the boat. The water started coming in and we ran her for shore.

A third of the way in the boat sank and we had to get out and get our assholes wet wading to shore. So the night ended up well and hadn't been wasted . . .

I played Nazi for some time longer, while caring for neither the Nazis nor the Communists nor the Americans. But I was losing interest. In fact, just before Pearl Harbor I gave it up. The fun had gone out of it. I felt the war was going to happen and I didn't feel much like going to war and I didn't feel much like being a conscientious objector either. It was catshit. It was useless. Me and my medium-sized cock were in trouble.

I sat in class without speaking, waiting. The students and the instructors needled me. I had lost my drive, my steam, my mox. I felt that the whole thing was out of my hands. It was going to happen. All the cocks were in trouble.

My English instructor, quite a nice lady with beautiful legs asked me to stay after class one day. "What's the matter, Chinaski?" she asked. "I've given up," I said. "You mean politics?" she asked. "I mean politics," I said. "You'd make a good sailor," she said. I walked out . . .

I was sitting with my best friend, a marine, in a downtown bar drinking a beer when it happened. A radio was playing music, there was a break in the music. They told us that Pearl Harbor had just been bombed. It was announced that all military personnel should return immediately to their bases. My friend asked that I take the bus with him to San Diego, suggesting that it might turn out to be the last time I ever saw him. He was right.

LOVE FOR $17.50

Robert's first desire—when he began thinking of such things—was to sneak into the Wax Museum some night and make love to the wax ladies. However, that seemed too dangerous. He limited himself to making love to statues and mannequins in his sex fantasies and lived in his fantasy world.

One day while stopped at a red light he looked into the doorway of a shop. It was one of those shops that sold everything—records, sofas, books, trivia, junk. He saw her standing there in a long red dress. She wore rimless glasses, was well-shaped; dignified and sexy the way they used to be. A real class broad. Then the signal changed and he was forced to drive on.

Robert parked a block away and walked back to the shop. He stood outside at the newspaper rack and looked in at her. Even the eyes looked real, and the mouth was very impulsive, pouting just a bit.

Robert went inside and looked at the record rack. He was closer to her then and sneaked glances. No, they didn't make them like that anymore. She even had on high heels.

The girl in the shop walked up. "Can I help you, sir?"

"Just browsing, miss."

"If there's anything you want, just let me know."

"Surely."

Robert moved over to the mannequin. There wasn't a price tag. He wondered if she were for sale. He walked back to the record rack, picked up a cheap album and purchased it from the girl.

The next time he visited the shop the mannequin was still there. Robert browsed a bit, bought an ashtray that was moulded to imitate a coiled snake, then walked out.

The third time he was there he asked the girl: "Is the mannequin for sale?"

"The mannequin?"

"Yes, the mannequin."

"You want to buy it?"

"Yes, you sell things, don't you? Is the mannequin for sale?"

"Just a moment, sir."

The girl went to the back of the shop. A curtain parted and an old Jewish man came out. The bottom two buttons of his shirt were missing and you could see his hairy belly. He seemed friendly enough.

"You want the mannequin, sir?"

"Yes, is she for sale?"

"Well, not really. You see, it's kind of a display piece, a joke."

"I want to buy her."

"Well, let's see . . ." The old Jew went over and began touching the mannequin, touching the dress, the arms. "Let's see . . . I think I can let you have this . . . thing . . . for $17.50."

"I'll take her." Robert pulled out a twenty. The storekeeper counted out the change.

"I'm going to miss it," he said, "sometimes it seems almost real. Should I wrap it?"

"No, I'll take her the way she is."

Robert picked up the mannequin and carried her to his car. He laid her down in the back seat. Then he got in and drove off to his place. When he got there, luckily, there didn't seem to be anybody about and he got her into the doorway unseen. He stood her in the center of the room and looked at her.

"Stella," he said, "Stella, bitch!"

He walked up and slapped her across the face. Then he grabbed the head and kissed it. It was a good kiss. His penis began to harden when the phone rang. "Hello," he answered.

"Robert?"

"Yeah. Sure."

"This is Harry."

"How you doing, Harry?"

"O.k., what you doing?"

"Nothing."

"I thought I'd come over. Bring a couple of beers."

"O.k."

Robert hung up, picked up the mannequin and carried her to the closet. He pushed her back in the corner of the closet and closed the door.

Harry really didn't have much to say. He sat there with his beer-can. "How's Laura?" he asked.

"Oh," said Robert, "it's all over between me and Laura."

"What happened?"

"The eternal vamp bit. Always on stage. She was relentless. She'd turn on for guys everywhere—at the grocery store, on the street, in cafes, everywhere and to anybody. It didn't matter who it was as long as it was a man. She even turned on for a guy who dialed a wrong number. I couldn't go it anymore."

"You alone now?"

"No, I've got another one. Brenda. You've met her."

"Oh yeah. Brenda. She's all right."

Harry sat there drinking beer. Harry never had a woman but he was always talking about them. There was something sickening about Harry. Robert didn't encourage the conversation and Harry soon left. Robert went to the closet and brought Stella out.

"You god damned whore!" he said. "You've been cheating on me, haven't you?"

Stella didn't answer. She stood there looking so cool and prim. He slapped her a good one. It'd be a long day in the sun before any woman got away with cheating on Bob Wilkenson. He slapped her another good one.

"Cunt! You'd fuck a four-year-old boy if he could get his pecker up, wouldn't you?"

He slapped her again, then grabbed her and kissed her. He kissed her again and again. Then he ran his hands up under her dress. She was well-shaped, very well-shaped. Stella reminded him of an algebra teacher he'd had in high school. Stella didn't have on panties.

"Whore," he said, "who got your panties?"

Then his penis was pressed against the front of her. There was no opening. But Robert was in a tremendous passion. He inserted it between the upper thighs. It was smooth and tight. He worked away. For just a moment he felt extremely foolish, then his passion took over and he began kissing her along the neck as he worked.

Robert washed Stella with a dishrag, placed her in the closet behind an overcoat, closed the door and still managed to get in the last quarter of the Detroit Lions vs. L.A. Rams game on T.V.

It was quite nice for Robert as time went on. He made certain adjustments. He bought Stella several pairs of underpants, a garter belt, sheer long stockings, an ankle bracelet.

He bought her earrings too, and was quite shocked to learn that his love didn't have any ears. Under all that hair, the ears were missing. He put the earrings on anyhow with adhesive tape. But there were advantages—he didn't have to take her to dinner, to parties, to dull movies; all those mundane things that meant so much to the average woman. And there were arguments. There would always be arguments, even with a mannequin. She wasn't talkative but he was sure she told him once, "You're the greatest lover of them all. That old Jew was a dull lover. You love with soul, Robert."

Yes, there were advantages. She wasn't like all the other women he had known. She didn't want to make love at inconvenient moments. He could choose the time. And she didn't have periods. And he went down on her. He cut some of the hair from her head and pasted it between her thighs.

The affair was sexual to begin with but gradually he was falling in love with her, he could feel it happening. He considered going to a psychiatrist, then decided not to. After all, was it necessary to love a real human being? It never lasted long. There were too many differences between the species, and what started as love too often ended up as war.

Then too, he didn't have to lie in bed with Stella and listen to her talk about all her past lovers. How Karl had such a big thing, but Karl wouldn't go down. And how Louie danced so well, Louie could have made it in ballet instead of selling insurance. And how Marty could really kiss. He had a way of locking tongues. So on. So forth. What shit. Of course, Stella had mentioned the old Jew. But just that once.

Robert had been with Stella about two weeks when Brenda phoned.

"Yes, Brenda?" he answered.

"Robert, you haven't phoned me."

"I've been terribly busy, Brenda. I've been promoted to district manager and I've had to realign things down at the office."

"Is that so?"

"Yes."

"Robert, something's wrong . . ."

"What do you mean?"

"I can tell by your voice. Something's wrong. What the hell's wrong, Robert? Is there another woman?"

"Not exactly."

"What do you mean, not exactly?"

"Oh, Christ!"

"What is it? What is it? Robert, something's wrong. I'm coming over to see you."

"There's nothing wrong, Brenda."

"You son of a bitch, you're holding out on me! Something's going on. I'm coming to see you! Now!"

Brenda hung up and Robert walked over and picked up Stella and put her in the closet, well back in one corner. He took the overcoat off the hanger and hung it over Stella. Then he came back, sat down and waited.

Brenda opened the door and rushed in. "All right, what the hell's wrong? What is it?"

"Listen, kid," he said, "it's o.k. Calm down."

Brenda was nicely built. Her breasts sagged a bit, but she had fine legs and a beautiful ass. Her eyes always had a frantic, lost look. He could never cure her eyes of that. Sometimes after lovemaking a temporary calm would fill her eyes but it never lasted.

"You haven't even kissed me yet!"

Robert got up from his chair and kissed Brenda.

"Christ, that was no kiss! What is it?" she asked. "What's wrong!"

"It's nothing, nothing at all . . ."

"If you don't tell me, I'm going to scream!"

"I tell you, it's nothing."

Brenda screamed. She walked to the window and screamed. You could hear her all over the neighborhood. Then she stopped.

"God, Brenda, don't do that again! Please, please!"

"I'll do it again! I'll do it again! Tell me what's wrong, Robert, or I'll do it again!"

"All right," he said, "wait."

Robert went to the closet, took the overcoat off Stella and lifted her out of the closet.

"What's that?" asked Brenda, "what's that?"

"A mannequin."

"A mannequin? You mean? . . ."

"I mean, I'm in love with her."

"Oh, my god! You mean? That thing? That *thing?*"

"Yes."

"You love that *thing* more than me? That hunk of celluloid, or whatever the shit she's made of? You mean you love that *thing* more than me?"

"Yes."

"I suppose you take it to bed with you? I suppose you do things to . . . with that *thing?*"

"Yes."

"Oh . . ."

Then Brenda really screamed. She just stood there and screamed. Robert thought she would never stop. Then she leaped at the mannequin and started to claw and beat at it. The mannequin toppled and fell against the wall. Brenda ran out the door, got in her car and drove off wildly. She crashed into the side of a parked car, glanced off, drove on.

Robert walked over to Stella. The head had broken off and rolled under a chair. There were spurts of chalky material on the floor. One arm hung loosely, broken, two wires protruding. Robert sat down in a chair. He just sat there. Then he got up and went into the bathroom, stood there a minute, and came back out. He stood in the hallway and could see the head under the chair. He began to sob. It was terrible. He didn't know what to do. He remembered how he had buried his mother and his father. But this was different. This was different. He just stood in the hallway, sobbing and waiting. Both of Stella's eyes were open and cool and beautiful. They stared at him.

A COUPLE OF WINOS

I was in my 20's and although I was drinking heavily and not eating, I was still strong. I mean, physically, and that's some luck for you when not much else is going right. My mind was in riot against my lot and life, and the only way I could calm it was to drink and drink and drink. I was walking up the road, it was dusty and dirty and hot, and I believe the state was California, but I'm no longer sure. It was desert land. I was walking along the road, my stockings hard and rotted and stinking, the nails were coming up through the soles of my shoes and into my feet and I had to keep cardboard in my shoes—cardboard, newspaper, anything that I could find. The nails worked through that, and you either got some more or you turned the stuff around, or upsidedown, or reshaped it.

The truck stopped alongside of me. I ignored it and kept walking. The truck started up again and the guy rode along beside me.

"Kid," the guy said, "you want a job?"

"Who've I got to kill?' I asked.

"Nobody," said the guy, "come on, get in."

I went around to the other side and when I got there the door was open. I stepped up on the running board, slid in, pulled the door shut and leaned back in the leather seat. I was out of the sun.

"You wanna suck me," said the guy, "you get five bucks."

I put the right hand hard into his gut, got the left somewhere in between the ear and the neck, came back with the right to the mouth and the truck ran off the road. I grabbed the wheel and steered it back. Then I cut the motor and braked. I climbed out and continued to walk along the road. About five minutes later the truck was running along next to me again.

"Kid," said the guy, "I'm sorry. I didn't mean that. I didn't mean you were a homo. I mean, though, you kind of half-look like a homo. Is there anything wrong with being a homo?"

"I guess if you're a homo there's not."

"Come on," said the guy, "get in. I got a real honest job for you. You can make some money, get on your feet."

I climbed in again. We drove off.

"I'm sorry," he said, "you got a real tough face, but look at your hands. You got ladies' hands."

"Don't worry about my hands," I said.

"Well, it's a tough job. Loadin' ties. You ever loaded ties?

"No."

"It's hard work."

"I've done hard work all my life."

"O.k.," said the guy, "o.k."

We drove along not talking, the truck rocking back and forth. There was nothing but dust, dust and desert. The guy didn't have much of a face, he didn't have much of anything. But sometimes small people who stay in the same place for a long time achieve minor prestige and power. He had the truck and he was hiring. Sometimes you have to go along with that.

We drove along and there was an old guy walking along the road. He must have been in his mid-forties. That's old for the road. This Mr. Burkhart, he'd told me his name, slowed his truck and asked the old guy. "Hey, buddy, you want to make a couple of bucks?"

"Oh, yes sir!" said the old guy.

"Move over. Let him in," said Mr. Burkhart.

The old guy got in and he really stank—of booze and sweat and agony and death. We drove on until we came to a small group of buildings. We got out with Burkhart and walked into a store. There was a guy in a green sunshade with a bunch of rubber bands around his left wrist. He was bald but his arms were covered with sickly long blond hair.

"Hello, Mr. Burkhart," he said, "I see you found yourself a couple more winos."

"Here's the list, Jesse," said Mr. Burkhart, and Jesse walked about filling orders. It took some time. Then he was finished. "Anything else, Mr. Burkhart? A couple cheap bottles of wine?"

"No wine for me," I said.

"O.k.," said the old guy, "I'll take both bottles."
"It'll come off your pay," Burkhart told the old guy.
"It doesn't matter," said the old guy, "take it off the pay."
"You sure you don't want a bottle?" Burkhart asked me.
"All right," I said, "I'll take a bottle."

We had a tent and that night we drank the wine and the old guy told me his troubles. He'd lost his wife. He still loved his wife. He thought about her all the time. A great woman. He used to teach mathematics. But he'd lost his wife. Never a woman like her. Blah blah blah.

Christ, when we woke up the old guy was sick and I wasn't feeling much better and the sun was up and out and we went to do our job: stacking railroad ties. You had to stack them into ricks. The bottom stacking was easy. But as we got higher we had to count. "One, two three," I'd count and then we'd let her go.

The old guy had a bandanna tied around his head and the booze poured out of his head and into the bandanna and the bandanna got soaked and dark. Every now and then a sliver from one of the railroad ties would knife through the rotten glove and into my hand. Ordinarily the pain would have been unbearable and I would have quit but fatigue dulled the senses, really properly dulled them. I just got angry when it happened—like I wanted to kill somebody, but when I looked around there was only sand and cliffs and the oven dry bright yellow sun and no place to go.

Every now and then the railroad company would rip up the old ties and replace them with new ones. They left the old ties laying beside the tracks. There wasn't much wrong with the old ties but the railroad left them laying around and Burkhart had guys like us stack them into ricks which he toted off in his truck and sold. I guess they had a lot of uses. On some of the ranches you'd see them stuck into the ground and strung with barbed wire and used as fences. I suppose there were other uses too. I wasn't much interested.

It was like any other impossible job, you got tired and you wanted to quit and then you got more tired and forgot to quit, and the minutes didn't move, you lived forever inside of one minute, no hope, no out, trapped, too dumb to quit and nowhere to go if you did quit.

"Kid, I lost my wife. She was such a wonderful woman. I keep thinking of her. A good woman is the greatest thing on earth."

"Yeh."

"If we only had a little wine."

"We don't have any wine. We gotta wait until tonight."

"I wonder if anybody understands winos?"

"Just other winos."

"Do you think those slivers in our hands will creep to our hearts?"

"No chance; we've never been lucky."

Two Indians came by and watched us. They watched us a long time. When the old guy and I sat down on a tie for a smoke one of the Indians walked over.

"You guys are doing it all wrong," he said.

"What do you mean?" I asked.

"You're working at the height of the desert heat. What you do is get up early in the morning and get your work done while it's cool."

"You're right," I said, "thanks."

The Indian was right. I decided we'd get up early. But we never made it. The old guy was always too sick from the night's drinking and I could never get him up on time.

"Five minutes more," he'd say, "just five minutes more."

Finally, one day, the old man gave out. He couldn't lift another tie. He kept apologizing about it.

"It's all right, Pops."

We got back to the tent and waited for evening. Pops layed there talking. He kept talking about his ex-wife. I heard about his ex-wife all through the day and into the evening. Then Burkhart arrived.

"Jesus Christ, you guys didn't do much today. You figure to live off the fat of the land?"

"We're through, Burkhart," I said, "we're waiting to get paid."

"I got a good mind not to pay you guys."

"If you got a good mind," I said, "you'll pay."

"Please, Mr. Burkhart," said the old guy, "please, please, we worked so god damned hard, honest we did!"

"Burkhart knows what we've done," I said, "he's got a count of the ricks and so have I."

"72 ricks," said Burkhart.

"90 ricks," I said.

"76 ricks," said Burkhart.
"90 ricks," I said.
"80 ricks," said Burkhart.
"Sold," I said.

Burkhart got out his pencil and paper and charged us for wine and food, transport and lodging. Pops and I each came up with $18 for five day's work. We took it. And got a free ride back to town. Free? Burkhart had fucked us from every angle. But we couldn't holler law because when you didn't have any money the law stopped working.

"By god," said the old guy, "I'm really going to get drunk. I'm going to get good and drunk. Aren't you, kid?"

"I don't think so."

We went into the only bar in town and sat down and Pops ordered a wine and I ordered a beer. The old guy started in on his ex-wife again and I moved down to the other end of the bar. A Mexican girl came down the stairway and sat down next to me. Why were they always coming down stairways like that, like in the movies? I even felt like I was in a movie. I bought her a beer. She said, "My name is Sherri," and I said, "That isn't Mexican," and she said, "It doesn't have to be," and I said, "You're right."

And it was five dollars upstairs and she washed me off first, and then later. She washed me off out of a little white bowl that had painted baby chickens chasing each other around the bowl. She made the same money in ten minutes that I had made in a day with some hours thrown in. Monetarily speaking, it seemed sure as shit you were better off having a pussy than a cock.

When I came down the stairway the old guy already had his head down on the bar; it had gotten to him. We hadn't eaten that day and he had no resistance. There was a dollar and some change by his head. For a moment I thought of taking him with me but I couldn't take care of myself. I walked outside. It was cool and I walked north.

I felt bad about leaving Pops there for the small town vultures. Then I wondered if the old guy's wife ever thought about him. I decided that she didn't, or if she did, it was hardly in the same way he thought about her. The whole earth crawled with sad hurt people like him. I needed a place to sleep. The bed I had been in with the Mexican girl had been the first I had been in for three weeks.

Some nights earlier I had found that when it got cold the slivers in my hand began to throb. I could feel where each one was. It began to get cold. I can't say that I hated the world of men and women, but I felt a certain disgust that separated me from the craftsmen and tradesmen and liars and lovers, and now decades later I feel that same disgust. Of course, this is only one man's story or one man's view of reality. If you'll keep reading maybe the next story will be happier. I hope so.

MAJA THURUP

It had gotten extensive press coverage and T.V. coverage and the lady was to write a book about it. The lady's name was Hester Adams, twice divorced, two children. She was 35 and one guessed that it was her last fling. The wrinkles were appearing, the breasts had been sagging for some time, the ankles and calves were thickening, there were signs of a belly. America had been taught that beauty only resided in youth, especially in the female. But Hester Adams had the dark beauty of frustration and upcoming loss; it crawled all over her, the upcoming loss, and it gave her a sexual something, like a desperate and fading woman sitting in a bar full of men. Hester had looked around, seen few signs of help from the American male, and had gotten onto a plane for South America. She had entered the jungle with her camera, her portable typewriter, her thickening ankles and her white skin and had gotten herself a cannibal, a black cannibal: Maja Thurup. Maja Thurup had a good look to his face. His face appeared to be written over with one thousand hangovers and one thousand tragedies. And it was true—he had had one thousand hangovers, but the tragedies all came from the same root: Maja Thurup was overhung, vastly overhung. No girl in the village would accept him. He had torn two girls to death with his instrument. One had been entered from the front, the other from the rear. No matter.

Maja was a lonely man and he drank and brooded over his loneliness until Hester Adams had come with guide and white skin and camera. After formal introductions and a few drinks by the fire, Hester had entered Maja's hut and taken all Maja Thurup could muster and had asked for more. It was a miracle for both of them and they were married in a three-day tribal ceremony, during which captured enemy tribesmen were roasted and consumed amid dancing, incantation, and drunkenness. It was after the ceremony, after the hangovers had cleared away that trouble began. The medicine man, having noted that Hester did not partake of the flesh of the roasted enemy tribesmen (garnished with pineapple, olives, and nuts) announced to one and all that this was not a white goddess, but one of the daughters of the evil god Ritikan. (Centuries ago Ritikan had been expelled from the tribal heaven for his refusal to eat anything but vegetables, fruits, and nuts.) This announcement caused dissension in the tribe and two friends of Maja Thurup were promptly murdered for suggesting that Hester's handling of Maja's overhang was a miracle in itself and the fact that she didn't ingest other forms of human meat could be forgiven—temporarily, at least.

Hester and Maja fled to America, to North Hollywood to be precise, where Hester began procedings to have Maja Thurup become an American citizen. A former schoolteacher, Hester began instructing Maja in the use of clothing, the English language, California beer and wines, television, and foods purchased at the nearby Safeway market. Maja not only looked at television, he appeared on it along with Hester and they declared their love publicly. Then they went back to their North Hollywood apartment and made love. Afterwards Maja sat in the middle of the rug with his English grammar books, drinking beer and wine, and singing native chants and playing the bongo. Hester worked on her book about Maja and Hester. A major publisher was waiting. All Hester had to do was get it down.

One morning I was in bed about 8:00 a.m. The day before I had lost $40 at Santa Anita, my savings account at California Federal was getting dangerously low, and I hadn't written a decent story in a month. The phone rang. I woke up, gagged, coughed, picked it up.

"Chinaski?"

"Yeah?"

"This is Dan Hudson."

Dan ran the magazine *Flare* out of Chicago. He paid well. He was the editor and publisher.

"Hello, Dan, mother."

"Look, I've got just the thing for you."

"Sure, Dan. What is it?"

"I want you to interview this bitch who married the cannibal. Make the sex BIG. Mix love with horror, you know?"

"I know. I've been doing it all my life."

"There's $500 in it for you if you beat the March 27 deadline."

"Dan, for $500, I can make Burt Reynolds into a lesbian."

Dan gave me the address and phone number. I got up, threw water on my face, had two Alka-Seltzers, opened a bottle of beer and phoned Hester Adams. I told her that I wanted to publicize her relationship with Maja Thurup as one of the great love stories of the 20th century. For the readers of *Flare* magazine. I assured her that it would help Maja obtain his American citizenship. She agreed to an interview at 1:00 p.m.

It was a walk-up apartment on the third floor. She opened the door. Maja was sitting on the floor with his bongo drinking a fifth of medium priced port from the bottle. He was barefooted, dressed in tight jeans, and in a white t-shirt with black zebra-stripes. Hester was dressed in an identical outfit. She brought me a bottle of beer, I picked up a cigarette from the pack on the coffee table and began the interview.

"You first met Maja when?"

Hester gave me a date. She also gave me the exact time and place.

"When did you first begin to have love feelings for Maja? What exactly were the circumstances which tripped them off?"

"Well," said Hester, "it was . . ."

"She love me when I give her the thing," said Maja from the rug.

"He has learned English quite quickly, hasn't he?"

"Yes, he's brilliant."

Maja picked up his bottle and drained off a good slug.

"I put this thing in her, she say, 'Oh my god oh my god oh my god!' Ha, ha, ha, ha!"

"Maja is marvelously built," she said.

"She eat too," said Maja, "she eat good. Deep throat, ha, ha, ha!"

"I loved Maja from the beginning," said Hester, "it was his eyes, his face . . . so tragic. And the way he walked. He walks, well, he walks something like a tiger."

"Fuck," said Maja, "we fuck we fucky fuck fuck fuck. I am getting tired."

Maja took another drink. He looked at me.
"You fuck her. I am tired. She big hungry tunnel."
"Maja has a genuine sense of humor," said Hester, "that's another thing that has endeared him to me."
"Only thing dear you to me," said Maja, "is my telephone pole piss-shooter."
"Maja has been drinking since this morning," said Hester, "you'll have to excuse him."
"Perhaps I'd better come back when he's feeling better."
"I think you should."
Hester gave me an appointment at 2:00 p.m. in the afternoon the next day.

It was just as well. I needed photographs. I knew a down-and-out photographer, one Sam Jacoby who was good and would do the work cheap. I took him back there with me. It was a sunny afternoon with only a thin layer of smog. We walked up and I rang. There was no answer. I rang again. Maja answered the door.
"Hester not in," he said, "she gone to grocery store."
"We had an appointment for 2:00 o'clock. I'd like to come in and wait."
We walked in and sat down.
"I play drums for you," said Maja.
He played the drums and sang some jungle chants. He was quite good. He was working on another bottle of port wine. He was still in his zebra-striped t-shirt and jeans.
"Fuck fuck fuck," he said, "that's all she want. She make me mad."
"You miss the jungle, Maja?"
"You just ain't just shittin' upstream, daddy."
"But she loves you, Maja."
"Ha, ha, ha!"
Maja played us another drum solo. Even drunk he was good.
When Maja finished Sam said to me, "You think she might have a beer in the refrigerator?"
"She might."
"My nerves are bad. I need a beer."
"Go ahead. Get two. I'll buy her some more. I should have brought some."
Sam got up and walked into the kitchen. I heard the refrigerator

door open.

"I'm writing an article about you and Hester," I said to Maja.

"Big-hole woman. Never fill. Like volcano."

I heard Sam vomiting in the kitchen. He was a heavy drinker. I knew he was hungover. But he was still one of the best photographers around. Then it was quiet. Sam came walking out. He sat down. He didn't have a beer with him.

"I play drums again," said Maja. He played the drums again. He was still good. Though not as good as the preceding time. The wine was getting to him.

"Let's get out of here," Sam said to me.

"I have to wait for Hester," I said.

"Man, let's go," said Sam.

"You guys want some wine?" asked Maja.

I got up and walked into the kitchen for a beer. Sam followed me. I moved toward the refrigerator.

"*Please* don't open that door!" he said.

Sam walked over to the sink and vomited again. I looked at the refrigerator door. I didn't open it. When Sam finished, I said, "O.k., let's go."

We walked into the front room where Maja still sat by his bongo.

"I play drum once more," he said.

"No, thanks, Maja."

We walked out and down the stairway and out to the street. We got into my car. I drove off. I didn't know what to say. Sam didn't say anything. We were in the business district. I drove into a gas station and told the attendant to fill it up with regular. Sam got out of the car and walked to the telephone booth to call the police. I saw Sam come out of the phone booth. I paid for the gas. I hadn't gotten my interview. I was out $500. I waited as Sam walked toward the car.

THE KILLERS

Harry had just gotten off the freight and was walking down Alameda toward Pedro's for a nickel cup of coffee. It was early morning but he remembered they used to open at 5 a.m. You could sit in Pedro's for a couple of hours for a nickel. You could do some thinking. You could remember where you'd gone wrong, or where you'd gone right.

They were open. The Mexican girl who gave him his coffee looked at him as if he were a human being. The poor knew life. A good girl. Well, a good enough girl. They all meant trouble. Everything meant trouble. He remembered a statement he'd heard somewhere: the Definition of Life is Trouble.

Harry sat down at one of the old tables. The coffee was good. Thirty-eight years old and he was finished. He sipped at the coffee and remembered where he had gone wrong—or right. He'd simply gotten tired—of the insurance game, of the small offices and high glass partitions, the clients; he'd simply gotten tired of cheating on his wife, of squeezing secretaries in the elevator and in the halls; he'd gotten tired of Christmas parties and New Year's parties and birthdays, and payments on new cars and furniture payments—light, gas, water—the whole bleeding complex of necessities.

He'd gotten tired and quit, that's all. The divorce came soon enough and the drinking came soon enough, and suddenly he was out of it. He had nothing, and he found out that having nothing was difficult too. It was another type of burden. If only there were some gentler road in between. It seemed a man only had two choices—get in on the hustle or be a bum.

As Harry looked up a man sat down across from him, also with a nickel cup of coffee. He appeared to be in his early forties. And was dressed as poorly as Harry. The man rolled a cigarette, then looked at Harry as he lit it.

"How's it going?"

"That's some question," said Harry.

"Yeah, I guess it is."

They sat drinking their coffee.

"A man wonders how he gets down here."

"Yeah," said Harry.

"By the way, if it matters, my name's William."

"I'm called Harry."

"You can call me Bill."

"Thanks."

"You got the look on your face like you've reached the end of something."

"I'm just tired of the bum, bone-tired."

"You want to get back into society, Harry?"

"No, not that. But I'd like to get out of this."

"There's suicide."

"I know."

"Listen," said Bill, "what we need is a little cash the easy way so we can get a breather."

"Sure, but how?"

"Well, there's some risk involved."

"Like what?"

"I used to do some house burglaring. It's not bad. I could use a good partner."

"O.k., I'm just about ready to try anything. I'm sick of watery beans, week-old doughnuts, the mission, the God-lectures, the snoring . . ."

"Our problem is how to get where we can operate," said Bill.

"I got a couple of bucks."

"All right, meet me about midnight. Got a pencil?"

"No."

"Wait. I'll borrow one."

Bill came back with a stub of pencil. He took a napkin and wrote on it.

"You take the Beverly Hills bus and ask the driver to let you off here. Then walk two blocks north. I'll be there waiting. You gonna make it?"

"I'll be there."

"You got a wife, kids?" asked Bill.
"Used to have," Harry answered.

It was cold that night. Harry got off the bus and walked the two blocks north. It was dark, very dark. Bill was standing smoking a rolled cigarette. He wasn't standing in the open but was back against a large bush.

"Hello, Bill."

"Hello, Harry. You ready to start your new lucrative career?"

"I am."

"All right. I've been casing these places. I think I've got us a good one. Isolated. It stinks of money. You scared?"

"No. I'm not scared."

"Fine. Be cool and follow me."

Harry followed Bill along the sidewalk for a block and a half, then Bill cut between two shrubs and onto a large lawn. They walked to the back of the house, a large two storey affair. Bill stopped at the rear window. He sliced the screen with a knife, then stood still and listened. It was like a graveyard. Bill unhooked the screen and lifted it off. He stood there working at the window. Bill worked at it for some time and Harry began to think: Jesus. I'm with an amateur. I'm with some kind of nut. Then the window opened and Bill climbed in. Harry could see his ass wiggling in. This is ridiculous, he thought. Do men do this?

"Come on," Bill said softly from inside.

Harry climbed in. It did stink of money and furniture polish.

"Jesus. Bill. I'm scared now. This doesn't make any sense."

"Don't talk so loud. You want to get away from those watery beans, don't you?"

"Yes."

"Well, then be a man."

Harry stood while Bill slowly opened drawers and put things in his pockets. They appeared to be in a dining room. Bill was stuffing spoons and knives and forks into his pockets.

How can we get anything for that? thought Harry.

Bill kept putting the silverware into his coat pockets. Then he dropped a knife. The floor was hard, without a rug, and the sound was definite and loud.

"Who's there?"

Bill and Harry didn't answer.

"I said, who's there?"

"What is it, Seymour?" said a girl's voice.

"I thought I heard something. Something woke me up."

"Oh go to sleep."

"No. I heard something."

Harry heard the sound of a bed and then the sound of a man walking. The man came through the door and was in the dining room with them. He was in his pajamas, a young man of about 26 or 27 with a goatee and long hair.

"All right, you pricks, what are you doing in my house?"

Bill turned toward Harry. "Get into that bedroom. There might be a phone there. See that she doesn't use it. I'll take care of this one."

Harry walked toward the bedroom, found the entrance, walked in, saw a young blonde about 23, long hair, in a fancy nightgown, her breasts loose. There was a telephone by the night stand and she wasn't using it. She flung the back of her hand to her mouth. She was sitting up in bed.

"Don't scream," said Harry, "or I'll kill you."

He stood there looking down at her, thinking of his own wife, but never a wife like that. Harry began to sweat, he felt dizzy and they stared at each other.

Harry sat down on the bed.

"Leave my wife alone or I'll kill you!" said the young man. Bill had just walked him in. He had an arm lock on him and his knife was poking into the middle of the young man's back.

"Nobody's going to hurt your wife, man. Just tell us where your stinking money is and we'll leave."

"I told you all I've got is what's in my wallet."

Bill tightened the arm lock and drove the knife in a bit. The young man winced.

"The jewelry," said Bill, "take me to the jewelry."

"It's upstairs . . ."

"All right. Take me there!"

Harry watched Bill walk him out. Harry kept staring at the girl and she stared back. Blue eyes, and the irises were large with fear.

"Don't scream," he told her, "or I'll kill you, so help me I'll kill you!"

Her lips began to tremble. They were the palest pink and then his mouth was upon hers. He was bewhiskered and foul, rancid, and she was white, soft white, delicate, trembling. He held her head in his hands. He pulled his head away and looked into her eyes. "You whore," he said, "you god damned whore!" He kissed her again, harder. They fell back on the bed together. He was kicking his shoes off, holding her down. Then he was working his pants, getting them off, and all the time holding and kissing her. "You whore, you god damned whore . . ."

"Oh No! Jesus Christ, No! Not my wife, you bastards!"

Harry had not heard them enter. The young man let out a scream. Then Harry heard a gurgle. He pulled out and looked around. The young man was on the floor with his throat cut; the blood spurted rhythmically out on the floor.

"You've killed him!" said Harry.

"He was screaming."

"You didn't have to kill him."

"You didn't have to rape his wife."

"I haven't raped her and you've killed him."

Then she began to scream. Harry put his hand over her mouth.

"What are we going to do?" he asked.

"We're going to kill her too. She's a witness."

"I can't kill her," said Harry.

"I'll kill her," said Bill.

"But we shouldn't waste her."

"Go ahead then, get her."

"Stick something in her mouth."

"I'll take care of it," said Bill. He got a scarf out of the drawer, stuck it in her mouth. Then he ripped the pillow slip into shreds and bound the scarf in.

"Go ahead," said Bill.

The girl didn't resist. She seemed to be in a state of shock.

When Harry got off, Bill got on. Harry watched. This was it. This was the way it worked all over the world. When a conquering army came in, they took the women. They were the conquering army.

Bill climbed off. "Shit, that sure was good."

"Listen, Bill, let's not kill her."

"She'll tell. She's a witness."

"If we spare her life, she won't tell. It'll be worth it to her."

"She'll tell. I know human nature. She'll tell later."

"Why shouldn't she tell on people who do what we do?"

"That's what I mean," said Bill, "why let her?"
"Let's ask her. Let's talk to her. Let's ask her what she thinks."
"I *know* what she thinks. I'm going to kill her."
"Please don't, Bill. Let's show some decency."
"Show some decency? Now? It's too late. If you'd only been man enough to keep your stupid pecker out of there . . ."
"Don't kill her, Bill, I can't . . . stand it . . ."
"Turn your back."
"Bill, please . . ."
"I said, turn your god damned back!"
Harry turned away. There didn't seem to be a sound. Minutes passed.
"Bill, did you do it?"
"I did it. Turn around and look."
"I don't want to. Let's go. Let's get out of here."
They went out the same window they had entered. The night was colder than ever. They went down the dark side of the house and out through the hedge.
"Bill?"
"Yeah?"
"I feel o.k. now, like it never happened."
"It happened."
They walked back toward the bus stop. The night stops were far between, they'd probably have to wait an hour. They stood at the bus stop and checked each other for blood and, strangely, they didn't find any. So they rolled and lit two cigarettes.
Then Bill suddenly spit his out.
"God damn it. Oh, god damn it all!"
"What's the matter, Bill?"
"We forgot to get his wallet!"
"Oh fuck," said Harry.

A MAN

George was lying in his trailer, flat on his back, watching a small portable T.V. His dinner dishes were undone, his breakfast dishes were undone, he needed a shave, and ash from his rolled cigarette dropped onto his undershirt. Some of the ash was still burning. Sometimes the burning ash missed the undershirt and hit his skin, then he cursed, brushing it away.

There was a knock on the trailer door. He got slowly to his feet and answered the door. It was Constance. She had a fifth of unopened whiskey in a bag.

"George, I left that son of a bitch, I couldn't stand that son of a bitch anymore."

"Sit down."

George opened the fifth, got two glasses, filled each a third with whiskey, two thirds with water. He sat down on the bed with Constance. She took a cigarette out of her purse and lit it. She was drunk and her hands trembled.

"I took his damn money too. I took his damn money and split while he was at work. You don't know how I've suffered with that son of a bitch."

"Lemme have a smoke," said George.

She handed it to him and as she leaned near, George put his arm around her, pulled her over and kissed her.

"You son of a bitch," she said, "I missed you."

"I missed those good legs of yours, Connie. I've really missed those good legs."

"You still like 'em?"

"I get hot just looking."

"I never could make it with a college guy," said Connie. "They're too soft, they're milktoast. And he kept his house clean. George, it was like having a maid. He did it all. The place was spotless. You could eat beef stew right out of the crapper. He was *antiseptic*, that's what he was."

"Drink up. You'll feel better."

"And he couldn't make love."

"You mean he couldn't get it up?"

"Oh, he got it up. He got it up all the time. But he didn't know how to make a woman happy, you know. He didn't know what to do. All that money, all that education—he was useless."

"I wish I had a college education."

"You don't need one. You've got everything you need, George."

"I'm just a flunky. All the shit jobs."

"I said you've got everything you need, George. You know how to make a woman happy."

"Yeh?"

"Yes. And you know what else? His *mother* came around! His *mother!* Two or three times a week. And she'd sit there looking at me, pretending to like me but all the time treating me like I was a whore. Like I was a big bad whore stealing her son away from her! Her precious Walter! Christ! What a mess!"

"Drink up, Connie."

George was finished. He waited for Connie to empty her glass, then took it, refilled both glasses.

"He claimed he loved me. And I'd say, 'Look at my pussy, Walter!' And he wouldn't look at my pussy. He said, 'I don't want to look at that thing.' That *thing!* That's what he called it! You're not afraid of my pussy, are you, George?"

"It's never bit me yet."

"But you've bit it, you've nibbled on it, haven't you, George?"

"I suppose I have."

"And you've licked it, sucked it?"

"I suppose so."

"You know damn well, George, what you've done."

"How much money did you get?"

"Six hundred dollars."

"I don't like people who rob other people, Connie."

"That's why you're a fucking dishwasher. You're honest. But he's such an ass, George. And he can afford the money, and I've earned it . . . him and his *mother* and his *love*, his *mother-love*, his clean little washbowls and toilets and disposal bags and new cars and breath chasers and after-shave lotions and his little hard-ons and his precious love-making. All for *himself*, you understand, all for *himself!* You know what a woman wants, George . . ."

"Thanks for the whiskey, Connie. Lemme have another cigarette.

George filled them up again. "I've missed your legs, Connie. I've really missed those legs. I like the way you wear those high-heels. They drive me crazy. These modern women don't know what they're missing. The high heel shapes the calf, the thigh, the ass; it puts rhythm into the walk. It really turns me on!"

"You talk like a poet, George. Sometimes you do talk like that. You are one hell of a dishwasher."

"You know what I'd really like to do?"

"What?"

"I'd like to whip you with my belt on the legs, the ass, the thighs. I'd like to make you quiver and cry and then when you're quivering and crying I'd slam it into you in pure love."

"I don't want that, George. You've never talked that way before. You've always done right with me."

"Pull your dress up higher."

"What?"

"Pull your dress up higher, I want to see more of your legs."

"You do like my legs, don't you, George?"

"Let the light shine on them!"

Constance hiked her dress.

"God Christ shit," said George.

"You like my legs?"

"I love your legs!"

Then George reached across the bed and slapped Constance hard across the face. Her cigarette flipped out of her mouth.

"What'd you do that for?"

"You fucked Walter! You fucked Walter!"

"So what the hell?"

"So pull your dress higher!"

"No!"

"Do what I say!"

George slapped her again, harder. Constance hiked her skirt.

"Just up to the panties!" shouted George. "I don't quite want to see the panties!"

"Christ, George, what's gone wrong with you?"
"You fucked Walter!"
"George, I swear, you've gone crazy. I want to leave. Let me out of here, George!"
"Don't move or I'll kill you!"
"You'd kill me?"
"I swear it!"
George got up and poured himself a full glass of straight whiskey, drank it, and sat down next to Constance. He took his cigarette and held it against her wrist. She screamed. He held it there, firmly, then pulled it away.
"I'm a man, baby, understand that?"
"I know you're a man, George."
"Here, look at my muscles!" George stood up and flexed both of his arms. "Beautiful, eh, baby? Look at that muscle! Feel it! Feel it!"
Constance felt one of his arms. Then the other.
"Yes, you have a beautiful body, George."
"I'm a man. I'm a dishwasher but I'm a man, a real man."
"I know it, George."
"I'm not like that milkshit you left."
"I know it."
"And I can sing too. You ought to hear my voice."
Constance sat there. George began to sing. He sang "Old Man River." Then he sang "Nobody Knows the Trouble I've Seen." He sang "The St. Louis Blues." He sang "God Bless America," stopping several times and laughing. Then he sat down next to Constance. He said, "Connie you have beautiful legs." He asked for another cigarette. He smoked it, drank two more drinks, then put his head down on Connie's legs, against the stockings, in her lap, and he said, "Connie, I guess I'm no good, I guess I'm crazy, I'm sorry I hit you, I'm sorry I burned you with that cigarette."
Constance sat there. She ran her fingers through George's hair, stroking him, soothing him. Soon he was asleep. She waited a while longer. Then she lifted his head and placed it on the pillow, lifted his legs and straightened them out on the bed. She stood up, walked to the fifth, poured a good jolt of whiskey into her glass, added a touch of water and drank it down. She walked to the trailer door, pulled it open, stepped out, closed it. She walked through the backyard, opened the fence gate, walked up the alley under the one

o'clock moon. The sky was clear of clouds. The same skyful of stars was up there. She got on the boulevard and walked east and reached the entrance of The Blue Mirror. She walked in, looked around and there was Walter sitting alone and drunk at the end of the bar. She walked up and sat down next to him.

"Missed me, baby?" she asked.

Walter looked up. He recognized her. He didn't answer. He looked at the bartender and the bartender walked toward them. They all knew each other.

CLASS

I am not sure where the place was. Somewhere north-east of California. Hemingway had just finished a novel, come in from Europe or somewhere, and he was in the ring fighting somebody. There were newspapermen, critics, writers—that tribe—and also some young ladies sitting in the ringside seats. I sat down in the last row. Most of the people weren't watching Hem. They were talking to each other and laughing.

The sun was up. It was some time in the early afternoon. I was watching Ernie. He had his man, was playing with him. He jabbed and crossed at will. Then he put the other fellow down. The people looked then. Hem's opponent was up at 8. Hem moved towards him, then stopped. Ernie pulled out his mouthpiece, laughed, waved his opponent off. It was too easy a kill. Ernie walked to his corner. He put his head back and somebody squeezed some water in his mouth.

I got up from my seat and walked slowly down the aisle between the seats. I reached up and rapped Hemingway on the side.

"Mr. Hemingway?"

"Yes, what is it?"

"I'd like to put on the gloves with you."

"Do you have any boxing experience?"

"No."

"Go get some."

"I'm here to kick your ass."

Ernie laughed. He said to the guy in the corner, "Get the kid into some trunks and gloves."

The guy jumped out of the ring and I followed him back up the aisle to the locker room.

"You crazy, kid?" he asked me.

"I don't know. I don't think so."

"Here. Try on these trunks."

"O.k."

"Oh, oh . . . they're too large."

"Fuck it. They're all right."

"O.k., let me tape your hands."

"No tape."

"No tape?"

"No tape."

"How about a mouthpiece?"

"No mouthpiece."

"You gonna fight in them shoes?"

"I'm gonna fight in them shoes."

I lit a cigar and followed him out. I walked down the aisle smoking a cigar. Hemingway climbed back into the ring and they put on his gloves. There was nobody in my corner. Finally somebody came over and put some gloves on me. We were called into the center of the ring for instructions.

"Now when you clinch," said the referee, "I'll . . .

"I don't clinch," I told the referee.

Other instructions followed.

"O.k., go back to your corners. And at the bell, come out fighting. May the better man win. And," he said to me, "you better take that cigar out of your mouth."

When the bell rang I came out with the cigar still in my mouth. Sucking in a mouthful of smoke, I blew it into Ernest Hemingway's face. The crowd laughed.

Hem moved in, jabbed and hooked, and missed both punches. I was fast on my feet. I danced a little jig, moved in, tap tap tap tap tap, five swift left jabs to Papa's nose. I glanced down at a girl in the front row, a very pretty thing, and just then Hem landed a right, smashing that cigar in my mouth. I felt it burn my mouth and cheek, and I brushed the hot ash off. I spit out the cigar stub and hooked one to Ernie's belly. He uppercut with a right and caught me on the ear with a left. He ducked under my right and caught me with a volley up against the ropes. Just at the bell he dropped me with a solid right to the chin. I got up and walked back to my corner.

A guy came over with a bucket.

"Mr. Hemingway wants to know if you'd care for another

round?" the guy asked me.

"You tell Mr. Hemingway that he was lucky. Smoke got in my eyes. One more round is all I need to do the job."

The guy with the bucket went over and I could see Hemingway laughing.

The bell rang and I came right out. I began landing, not too hard but with good combinations. Ernie retreated, missing his punches. For the first time I saw doubt in his eyes.

Who is this kid?, he was thinking. I shortened my punches, hit him harder. I landed with every blow. Head and body. A mixed variety. I boxed like Sugar Ray and hit like Dempsey.

I had Hemingway up against the ropes. He couldn't fall. Each time he started to fall forward I straightened him with another punch. It was murder. *Death in the Afternoon.*

I stepped back and Mr. Ernest Hemingway fell forward, out cold.

I unlaced my gloves with my teeth, pulled them off, and leaped from the ring. I walked to my dressing room, I mean Hemingway's dressing room, and took a shower. I drank a bottle of beer, lit a cigar, and sat on the edge of the rubbing table. They carried Ernie in and put him on another table. He was still out. I sat there naked, watching them worry over Ernie. There were women in the room but I didn't pay any attention. Then a guy came over.

"Who are you?" he asked. "What's your name?"

"Henry Chinaski."

"Haven't heard of you," he said.

"You will," I said.

All the people came over. Ernie was left alone. Poor Ernie. Everybody crowded around me. The women too. I was pretty starved-down, except for one place. A real class broad was really looking me up and down. She looked like a society broad, rich, educated, and everything—nice body, nice face, nice clothes, all that.

"What do you do?" somebody asked me.

"Fuck and drink."

"No, no, I mean what's your occupation?"

"Dishwasher."

"Dishwasher?"

"Yeah."

"Do you have a hobby?"

"Well, I don't know if you could call it a hobby. I write."

"You write?"
"Yeh."
"What?"
"Short stories. They're pretty good."
"Have you been published?"
"No."
"Why?"
"I haven't submitted."
"Where are your stories?"
"Over there," I pointed to a torn paper suitcase.
"Listen, I'm a critic for *The New York Times*. Do you mind if I take your stories home and read them? I'll return them."
"It's o.k. with me, punk, only I don't know where I'll be."
The class society broad stepped forward. "He'll be with me."
Then she said, "Come on, Henry, get into your togs. It's a long drive in and we have things to—talk about."
I got dressed and then Ernie regained consciousness.
"What the hell happened?" he asked.
"You met a pretty good man, Mr. Hemingway," somebody told him.
I finished dressing and went over to his table.
"You're a good man, Papa. Nobody wins them all." I shook his hand. "Don't blow your brains out."
I left with the society broad and we got into an open-topped yellow car half a block long. She drove with the throttle to the floor and took the curves sliding and screeching and without expression. That was class. If she loved like she drove it was going to be a hell of a night.

The place was up in the hills, off by itself. A butler opened the door.
"George," she told him, "take the night off. On second thought, take the week off."
We walked in and there was a big guy sitting in a chair with a drink in his hand.
"Tommy," she said, "get lost."
We moved on through the house.
"Who was the big guy?" I asked her.
"Thomas Wolfe," she said, "a bore."
She stopped in the kitchen for a fifth of bourbon and two glasses.

Then she said, "Come on."
I followed her into the bedroom.

The next morning the phone awakened us. It was for me. She handed me the phone and I sat up in bed next to her.
"Mr. Chinaski?"
"Yeh?"
"I read your stories. I was so excited that I couldn't sleep all night. You're surely the greatest genius of the decade!"
"Only of the decade?"
"Well, perhaps of the century."
"That's better."
"The editors of *Harper's* and *Atlantic* are here with me now. You may not believe this but each of them has accepted five stories for future publication."
"I believe it," I said.
The critic hung up. I lay down. The society broad and I made love one more time.

STOP STARING AT MY TITS, MISTER

Big Bart was the meanest man in the West. He had the fastest gun in the West and he'd fucked a larger variety of women in the West than anybody else. He wasn't fond of bathing or bullshit or coming out second best. He was also boss of a wagon train going West, and there wasn't a man his age who had killed more Indians or fucked more women or killed more white men.

Big Bart was great and he knew it and everybody knew it. Even his farts were exceptional, louder than the dinner gong, and he was well-hung. Big Bart's gig was to get the wagons through safely, score on the ladies, kill a few men and then head back for another wagon load. He had a black beard, a dirty bunghole, and radiant yellow teeth.

He had just hammered hell out of Billy Joe's young wife while he made Billy Joe watch. He made Billy Joe's wife talk to Billy Joe while he was at it. He made her say, "Ah, Billy Joe, all this turkeyneck stuck into me from snatch to throat, I can hardly breathe! Billy Joe, save me! No, Billy Joe, don't save me!"

After Big Bart climaxed he made Billy Joe wash his parts and then they all went out to a big dinner of hamhocks and limas with biscuits.

The next day they came across this lone wagon running all by itself through the prairie. Some skinny kid of about sixteen with a bad case of acne was at the reins. Big Bart rode over.

"Say, kid," he said.

The kid didn't answer.

"I'm talkin' to ya, kid . . ."

"Kiss my ass," said the kid.

"I'm Big Bart," said Big Bart.

"Kiss my ass, Big Bart," said the kid.

"What's your name, son?"

"They call me 'The Kid.' "

"Look, Kid, there's no way a man can make it through this here Indian territory with a lone wagon."

"I intend to," said the Kid.

"O.k., it's your balls, Kid," said Big Bart, and he made to ride off when the flaps of the wagon opened and out came this little filly with 40-inch breasts and a fine big ass and eyes like the sky after a good rain. She put her eyes upon Big Bart and his turkeyneck quivered against the saddle horn.

"For your own good, Kid, you're a comin' with us."

"Fuck off, old man," said The Kid, "I don't take no motherfuckin' advice from an old man in dirty underwear."

"I've killed men for blinkin their eyes," said Big Bart.

The Kid just spit on the ground. Then reached up and scratched his crotch.

"Old man, you bore me. Now lose yourself from my sight or I'll assist you in resembling a hunk of swiss cheese."

"Kid," said the girl, leaning over him, one of her breasts flopping out and giving the sunlight a hard-on, "Kid, I think the man's right. We got no chance against those motherfucking Indians alone. Now don't be an asshole. Tell the man we'll join up."

"We'll join up," said The Kid.

"What's your girl's name?" asked Big Bart.

"Honeydew," said The Kid.

"And stop staring at my tits, mister," said Honeydew, "or I'll belt the shit out of you."

Things went well for a while. There was a skirmish with the Indians at Blueball Canyon. 37 Indians killed, one captured. No American casualties. Big Bart bungholed the captured Indian and then hired him on as cook. There was another skirmish at Clap Canyon, 37 Indians killed, one captured. No American casualties. Big Bart bungholed . . .

It was obvious that Big Bart had hotrocks for Honeydew. He couldn't keep his eyes off her. That ass, mostly it was that ass. He fell off his horse watching one time and one of the two Indian cooks laughed. That left only one Indian cook.

One day Big Bart sent The Kid out with a hunting party to score on some buffalo. Big Bart waited until they rode off and then he made for The Kid's wagon. He leaped up onto the seat and pushed the flaps back and walked in. Honeydew was crouched in the center of the wagon masturbating.

"Jesus, baby," said Big Bart, "don't waste it!"

"Get the hell out of here," said Honeydew, withdrawing her finger and pointing it at Big Bart, "get the hell out of here and let me do my thing!"

"Your man ain't takin' care of you, Honeydew!"

"He's takin' care of me, asshole, it's just that I don't get enough. It's just that after my period I get hot."

"Listen, baby . . ."

"Fuck off!"

"Listen, baby, lookee . . ."

And he pulled out the jackhammer. It was purple and flipped back and forth like the weight in a grandfather's clock. Driblets of spittle fell to the floor.

Honeydew couldn't keep her eyes off that instrument. At last she said, "You're not going to stick that god damned thing into me!"

"Say it like you mean it, Honydew."

"YOU'RE NOT GOING TO STICK THAT GOD DAMNED THING INTO ME!"

"But why? Why? Look at it!"

"I am looking at it!"

"But why don't you want it?"

"Because I'm in love with The Kid."

"Love?" said Big Bart laughing. "Love? That's a fairytale for idiots! Look at this god damned scythe! That can beat love anytime!"

"I love The Kid, Big Bart."

"And there's my tongue," said Big Bart, "the best tongue in the West!"

He stuck it out and made it do gymnastics.

"I love The Kid," said Honeydew.

"Well, fuck you," said Big Bart, and he ran forward and threw himself upon Honeydew. It was dog's work getting that thing in and when he did, Honeydew screamed. He gave it about seven slices and then he felt himself being roughly pulled off.

IT WAS THE KID. BACK FROM THE HUNTING PARTY.

"We got your buffalo, motherfucker. Now if you'll pull up your pants and step outside we'll settle the rest."

"I've got the fastest gun in the West," said Big Bart.

"I'll blow a hole in you so big your asshole will look like a pore in your skin," said The Kid. "Come on, let's get it done. I'm hungry for dinner. This hunting buffalo works up the appetite . . ."

The men sat around the campfire watching. There was a definite vibration in the air. The women stayed in the wagons, praying, masturbating, and drinking gin. Big Bart had 34 notches in his gun, and a bad memory. The Kid didn't have any notches in his gun. But he had confidence such as the others had seldom seen before. Big Bart seemed the more nervous of the two. He took a sip of whiskey, draining half the flask, then walked up to The Kid.

"Look, Kid . . ."

"Yeah, motherfucka . . .?"

"I mean, why you lost your cool?"

"I'm gonna blow your balls off, old man!"

"What for?"

"You were messin' with my woman, old man!"

"Listen Kid, don't you see? The female plays one man against the other. We're just falling for her game."

"I don't want to hear your shit, dad! Now back off and draw! You've had it!"

"Kid . . ."

"Back off and draw!"

The men at the campfire stiffened. A slight wind blew from the West smelling of horseshit. Somebody coughed. The women crouched in the wagons, drinking gin, praying, and masturbating. Twilight was moving in.

Big Bart and The Kid were 30 paces apart.

"Draw, you chickenshit," said The Kid, "draw, you chickenshit woman molester!"

Quietly through the flaps of a wagon a woman appeared with a rifle. It was Honeydew. She put the rifle to her shoulder and squinted down the barrel.

"Come on, you tinhorn rapist," said The Kid, "DRAW!"

Big Bart's hand flicked toward his holster. A shot rang through the twilight. Honeydew lowered her smoking rifle and went back into the covered wagon. The Kid was dead on the ground, a hole in his forehead. Big Bart put his unused gun back in his holster and strode toward the wagon. The moon was up.

SOMETHING ABOUT A VIET CONG FLAG

The desert baked under the summer sun. Red jumped off the freight as it slowed just outside the railroad yard. He took a shit behind some tall rocks to the north, wiped his ass with some leaves. Then he walked fifty yards, sat behind another rock out of the sun and rolled a cigarette. He saw the hippies walking toward him. Two guys and a girl. They had jumped off the train in the yard and were walking back.

One of the guys carried a Viet Cong flag. The guys looked soft and harmless. The girl had a nice wide ass—it almost split her bluejeans. She was blond and had a bad case of acne. Red waited until they almost reached him.

"Heil Hitler!" he said.

The hippies laughed.

"Where you going?" Red asked.

"We're trying to get to Denver. I guess we'll make it."

"Well," said Red, "you're going to have to wait a while. I'm going to have to use your girl."

"What do you mean?"

"You heard me."

Red grabbed the girl. With one hand grabbing her hair and the other her ass, he kissed her. The taller of the guys reached for Red's shoulder. "Now wait a minute . . ."

Red turned and put the guy on the ground with a short left. A stomach punch. They guy stayed down, breathing heavily. Red looked at the guy with the Viet Cong flag. "If you don't want to get hurt, leave me alone."

"Come on," he said to the girl, "get over behind those rocks."

"No, I won't do it," said the girl, "I won't do it."

Red pulled his switchblade and hit the button. The blade was flat across her nose, pressed it down.

"How do you think you'd look without a nose?"

She didn't answer.

"I'll slice it off." He grinned.

"Listen," said the guy with the flag, "you can't get away with this."

"Come on, girly," said Red, pushing her toward the rocks.

Red and the girl disappeared behind the rocks. The guy with the flag helped his friend up. They stood there. They stood there some minutes.

"He's fucking Sally. What can we do? He's fucking her right now."

"What can we do? He's a madman."

"We should do something."

"Sally must think we're real shits."

"We are. There are two of us. We could have handled him."

"He has a knife."

"It doesn't matter. We could have taken him."

"I feel god damned miserable."

"How do you think Sally feels? He's fucking her."

They stood and waited. The tall one who had taken the punch was called Leo. The other was Dale. It was hot in the sun as they waited. "We've got two cigarettes left," said Dale, "should we smoke?"

"How the hell can we smoke when that's going on behind the rocks?"

"You're right. My god, what's taking so long."

"God, I don't know. You think he's killed her?"

"I'm getting worried."

"Maybe I'd better have a look."

"O.k. but be careful."

Leo walked toward the rocks. There was a small hill with some brush. He crawled up the hill behind the brush and looked down. Red was fucking Sally. Leo watched. It seemed endless. Red went on and on. Leo crawled down the hill and walked over and stood next to Dale.

"I guess she's all right," he said.

They waited.

Finally Red and Sally came out from behind the rocks. They

walked toward them.

"Thank you brothers," said Red, "she was a very fine piece."

"May you rot in hell!" said Leo.

Red laughed. "Peace! Peace! . . . He flashed the sign with his fingers. "Well, I think I'll be going . . ."

Red rolled a quick cigarette, smiling as he wet it. Then he lit up, inhaled, and walked off toward the north, keeping in the shade.

"Let's hitchhike the rest of the way," said Dale. "Freights aren't any good."

"The highway's to the west," said Leo, "let's go."

They began moving toward the west.

"Christ,' said Sally, "I can hardly walk! He's an animal!"

Leo and Dale didn't say anything.

"I hope I don't get pregnant," said Sally.

"Sally," said Leo, "I'm sorry . . ."

"Oh, shut up!"

They walked. It was getting along toward evening and the desert heat was dropping off.

"I hate men!" said Sally.

A jackrabbit leaped out from behind a bush and Leo and Dale jumped as it ran off.

"A rabbit," said Leo, "a rabbit."

"That rabbit scared you guys, didn't it?"

"Well, after what happened, we're jumpy."

"*You're* jumpy? What about me? Listen let's sit down a minute. I'm tired."

There was a patch of shade and Sally sat between them.

"You know, though . . . " she said.

"What?"

"It wasn't so bad. On a strictly sexual basis, I mean. He really put it to me. On a strictly sexual basis it was quite something."

"What?" said Dale.

"I mean, morally, I hate him. The son of a bitch should be shot. He's a dog. A pig. But on a strictly sexual basis it was something . . ."

They sat there a while not saying anything. Then they got out the two cigarettes and smoked them, passing them around.

"I wish we had some dope," said Leo.

"God, I knew it was coming, said Sally. "You guys almost don't exist."

"Maybe you'd feel better if we raped you?" asked Leo.

"Don't be stupid."

"You think I can't rape you?"

"I should have gone with him. You guys are nothing."

"So now you like him?" asked Dale.

"Forget it!" said Sally. "Let's get down to the highway and stick our thumbs out."

"I can slam it to you," said Leo, "I can make you cry."

"Can I watch?" asked Dale, laughing.

"There won't be anything to watch," said Sally. "Come on. Let's go."

They stood up and walked toward the highway. It was a ten minute walk. When they got there Sally stood in the highway with her thumb out. Leo and Dale stood back out of view. They had forgotten the Viet Cong flag. They had left it back at the freight yard. It was in the dirt near the railroad tracks. The war went on. Seven red ants, the big kind, crawled across the flag.

YOU CAN'T WRITE A LOVE STORY

Margie was going to go out with this guy but on the way over this guy met another guy in a leather coat and the guy in the leather coat opened the leather coat and showed the other guy his tits and the other guy went over to Margie's and said he couldn't keep his date because this guy in the leather coat had showed him his tits and he was going to fuck this guy. So Margie went to see Carl. Carl was in, and she sat down and said to Carl, "This guy was going to take me to a café with tables outside and we were going to drink wine and talk, just drink wine and talk, that's all, nothing else, but on the way over this guy met another guy in a leather coat and the guy in the leather coat showed the other guy his tits and now this guy is going to fuck the guy in the leather coat, so I don't get my table and my wine and my talk."

"I can't write," said Carl. "It's gone."

Then he got up and went to the bathroom, closed the door, and took a shit. Carl took four or five shits a day. There was nothing else to do. He took five or six baths a day. There was nothing else to do. He got drunk for the same reason.

Margie heard the toilet flush. Then Carl came out.

"A man simply can't write eight hours a day. He can't even write every day or every week. It's a wicked fix. There's nothing to do but wait."

Carl went to the refrigerator and came out with a six-pack of Michelob. He opened a bottle.

"I'm the world's greatest writer," he said. "Do you know how difficult that is?"

Margie didn't answer.

"I can feel pain crawling all over me. It's like a second skin. I wish I could shed that skin like a snake."

"Well, why don't you get down on the rug and give it a try?"

"Listen," he asked, "where did I meet you?"

"Barney's Beanery."

"Well, that explains some of it. Have a beer."

Carl opened a bottle and passed it over.

"Yeah," said Margie, "I know. You need your solitude. You need to be alone. Except when you want some, or except when we split, then you're on the phone. You say you need me. You say you're dying of a hangover. You get weak fast."

"I get weak fast."

"And you're so *dull* around me, you never turn on. You writers are so . . . *precious* . . . you can't stand people. Humanity stinks, right?"

"Right."

"But every time we split you start throwing giant four-day parties. And suddenly you get *witty*, you start to TALK! Suddenly you're full of life, talking, dancing, singing. You dance on the coffeetable, you throw bottles through the window, you act parts from Shakespeare. Suddenly you're alive—when I'm gone. Oh, I hear about it!"

"I don't like parties. I especially dislike people at parties."

"For a guy who doesn't like parties you certainly throw enough of them."

"Listen, Margie, you don't understand. I can't write anymore. I'm finished. Somewhere I made a wrong turn. Somewhere I died in the night."

"The only way you're going to die is from one of your giant hangovers."

"Jeffers said that even the strongest men get trapped."

"Who was Jeffers?"

"He was the guy who turned Big Sur into a tourist trap."

"What were you going to do tonight?"

"I was going to listen to the songs of Rachmaninoff."

"Who's that?"

"A dead Russian."

"Look at you. You just sit there."

"I'm waiting. Some guys wait for two years. Sometimes it never comes back."

"Suppose it never comes back?"

"I'll just put on my shoes and walk down to Main Street."

"Why don't you get a decent job?"

"There aren't any decent jobs. If a writer doesn't make it through creation, he's dead."

"Oh, come on, Carl! There are billions of people in the world who don't make it through creation. Do you mean to tell me they're dead?"

"Yes."

"And you have soul? You are one of the few with a soul?"

"It would appear so."

"It would *appear* so! You and your little typewriter! You and your tiny checks! My grandmother makes more money than you do!"

Carl opened another bottle of beer.

"Beer! Beer! You and your god damned beer! It's in your stories too. 'Marty lifted his beer. As he looked up, this big blonde walked into the bar and sat down beside him . . .' You're right. You're finished. Your material is limited, very limited. You can't write a love story, you can't write a decent love story."

"You're right, Margie."

"If a man can't write a love story, he's useless."

"How many have you written?"

"I don't claim to be a writer."

"But," said Carl, "you appear to pose as one hell of a literary critic."

Margie left soon after that. Carl sat and drank the remaining beers. It was true, the writing had left him. It would make his few underground enemies happy. They could step one notch up. Death pleased them, underground or overground. He remembered Endicott, Endicott sitting there saying, "Well, Hemingway's gone, Dos Passos is gone, Patchen is gone, Pound is gone, Berryman jumped off the bridge . . . things are looking better and better and better."

The phone rang. Carl picked it up. "Mr. Gantling?"

"Yes?" he answered.

"We wondered if you'd like to read at Fairmount College?"

"Well, yes, what date?"

"The 30th of next month."

"I don't think I'm doing anything then."

"Our usual payment is one hundred dollars."

"I usually get a hundred and a half. Ginsberg gets a thousand."

"But that's Ginsberg. We can only offer a hundred."
"All right."
"Fine, Mr. Gantling. We'll send you the details."
"How about travel? That's a hell of a drive."
"O.k., twenty-five dollars for travel."
"O.k."
"Would you like to talk to some of the students in their classes?"
"No."
"There's a free lunch."
"I'll take that."
"Fine, Mr. Gantling, we'll be looking forward to seeing you on campus."
"Goodbye."

Carl walked about the room. He looked at the typewriter. He put a sheet of paper in there, then watched a girl in an amazingly short mini skirt walk past the window. Then he started to type:

"Margie was going to go out with this guy but on the way over this guy met another guy in a leather coat and the guy in the leather coat opened the leather coat and showed the other guy his tits and the other guy went over to Margie's and said he couldn't keep his date because this guy in the leather coat had showed him his tits . . ."

Carl lifted his beer. It felt good to be writing again.

REMEMBER PEARL HARBOR?

We got to go to the exercise yard twice a day, in the middle of the morning and in mid-afternoon. There wasn't much to do. The men were friends mostly on the basis of what had gotten them into jail. Like my cell-mate Taylor had said, the child molestors and indecent exposure cases were at the bottom of the social order while the big-time swindlers and the racket heads were at the top.

Taylor wouldn't speak to me in the exercise yard. He paced up and down with a big-time swindler. I sat alone. Some of the guys rolled a shirt into a ball and played catch. They appeared to enjoy it. The facilities for the entertainment of the inmates didn't amount to much.

I sat there. Soon I noticed a huddle of men. It was a crap game. I got up and went over. I had a little less than a dollar in change. I watched a few rolls. The man with the dice picked up three pots in a row. I sensed that his run was finished and got in against him. He crapped out. I made a quarter.

Each time a man got hot I laid off until I figured his string was ended. Then I got in against him. I noticed that the other men bet every pot. I made six bets and won five of them. Then we were marched back up to our cells. I was a dollar ahead.

The next morning I got in earlier. I made $2.50 in the morning and $1.75 in the afternoon. As the game ended this kid walked up to me. "You seem to be going all right, mister."

I gave the kid 15 cents. He walked off ahead. Another guy got in step with me. "You give that son of a bitch anything?"

"Yeah. 15 cents."

"He cuts the pot each time. Don't give him nothing."

"I hadn't noticed."

"Yeah. He cuts the pot. He takes his cut each roll."

"I'll watch him tomorrow."

"Besides, he's a fucking indecent exposure case. He shows his pecker to little girls."

"Yeah," I said, "I hate those cocksuckers."

The food was very bad. After dinner one night I mentioned to Taylor that I was winning at craps.

"You know," he said, "you can buy food here, good food."

"How?"

"The cook comes down after lights out. You get the warden's food, the best. Dessert, the works. The cook's good. The warden's got him here on account of that."

"How much would a couple of dinners cost us?"

"Give him a dime. No more than 15 cents."

"Is that all?"

"If you give him more he'll think you're a fool."

"All right. 15 cents."

Taylor made the arrangements. The next night after lights out we waited and killed bedbugs, one by one.

"That cook's killed two men. He's a great big son of a bitch, and mean. He killed one guy, did ten years, got out of there and was out two or three days and he killed another guy. This is only a holding prison but the warden keeps him here permanent because he's such a good cook."

We heard somebody walking up. It was the cook. I got up and he passed the food in. I walked to the table then walked back to the cell door. He was a big son of a bitch, killer of two men. I gave him 15 cents.

"Thanks, buddy, you want me to come back tomorrow night?"

"Every night."

Taylor and I sat down to the food. Everything was on plates. The coffee was good and hot, the meat—the roast beef—was tender. Mashed potatoes, sweet peas, biscuits, gravy, butter, and apple pie. I hadn't eaten that good in five years.

"That cook raped a sailor the other day. He got him so bad the sailor couldn't walk. They had to hospitalize that sailor."

I took in a big mouthful of mashed potatoes and gravy.

"You don't have to worry," said Taylor. "You're so damned ugly, nobody would want to rape you."

"I was worrying more about getting myself a little."

"Well, I'll point out the punks to you. Some of them are owned and some of them aren't owned."

"This is good food."

"Sure as shit. Now there are two kinds of punks in here. The kind that come in punks and the prison-made punks. There are never enough punks to go around so the boys have to make a few extra to fulfill their needs."

"That's sensible."

"The prison-manufactured punks are usually a little punchy from the head-beatings they take. They resist at first."

"Yeah?"

"Yeah. Then they decide it's better to be a live punk than a dead virgin."

We finished our dinner, went to our bunks, fought the bedbugs and attempted to sleep.

I continued to win at craps each day. I bet more heavily and still won. Life in prison was getting better and better. One day I was told not to go to the exercise yard. Two agents from the F.B.I. came to visit me. They asked a few questions, then one of them said: "We've investigated you. You don't have to go to court. You'll be taken to the induction center. If the army accepts you, you'll go in. If they reject you, you're a civilian again."

"I almost like it here in jail," I said.

"Yes, you're looking good."

"No tension," I said, "no rent, no utility bills, no arguments with girlfriends, no taxes, no license plates, no food bills, no hangovers . . ."

"Keep talking smart, we'll fix you good."

"Oh shit," I said, "I'm just joking. Pretend I'm Bob Hope."

"Bob Hope's a good American."

"I'd be too if I had his dough."

"Keep mouthing. We can make it rough on you."

I didn't answer. One guy had a briefcase. He got up first. The other guy followed him out.

They gave us all a bag lunch and put us in a truck. There were twenty or twenty-five of us. The guys had just had breakfast an hour and a half earlier but they were all into their bag lunches.

Not bad: a bologna sandwich, a peanut butter sandwich and a rotten banana. I passed my lunch down to the guys. They were very quiet. None of them joked. They looked straight ahead. Most of them were black or brown. And all of them were big.

I passed the physical, then I went in to see the psychiatrist.

"Henry Chinaski?"

"Yes."

"Sit down."

I sat down.

"Do you believe in the war?"

"No."

"Are you willing to go to war?"

"Yes."

He looked at me. I stared down at my feet. He seemed to be reading a sheaf of papers in front of him. It took several minutes. Four, five, six, seven minutes. Then he spoke.

"Listen, I am having a party next Wednesday night at my place. There are going to be doctors, lawyers, artists, writers, actors, all that sort. I can see that you're an intelligent man. I want you to come to my party. Will you come?"

"No."

He started writing. He wrote and he wrote and he wrote. I wondered how he knew so much about me. I didn't know that much about myself.

I let him write on. I was indifferent. Now that I couldn't be in the war I almost wanted the war. Yet, at the same time, I was glad to be out of it. The Doctor finished writing. I felt I had fooled them. My objection to war was not that I had to kill somebody or be killed senselessly, that hardly mattered. What I objected to was to be denied the right to sit in a small room and starve and drink cheap wine and go crazy in my own way and at my own leisure.

I didn't want to be awakened by some man with a bugle. I didn't want to sleep in a barracks with a bunch of healthy sex-mad football-loving overfed wise-cracking masturbating lovable frightened pink farting mother-struck modest basketball-playing American boys that I would have to be friendly with, that I would have to get drunk with on leave, that I would have to lay on my back with and listen to dozens of unfunny, obvious, dirty jokes. I didn't want their itchy blankets or their itchy uniforms or their itchy humanity. I didn't want to shit in the same place or piss in the same place or share the same whore. I didn't want to see their toenails or read their letters from home. I didn't want to watch their assholes bobbing in front of me in close formation, I didn't want to make friends, I didn't want to make enemies, I just didn't want them or it or the thing. To kill or be killed hardly mattered.

After a two-hour wait on a hard bench in a cesspool-brown tunnel with a cold wind blowing they let me go and I walked out, north. I stopped for a pack of cigarettes. I stopped in at the first bar, sat down, ordered a scotch and water, peeled the cellophane from the package, took out a smoke, lit up, got that drink in my hand, drank down half, dragged at the smoke, looked at my handsome face in the mirror. It seemed strange to be out. It seemed strange to be able to walk in any direction I pleased.

Just for fun I got up and walked to the crapper. I pissed. It was another horrible bar crapper; I almost vomited at the stench. I came out, put a coin in the juke box, sat down and listened to the latest. The latest wasn't any better. They had the beat but not the soul. Mozart, Bach and the Bee still made them look bad. I was going to miss those crap games and the good food. I ordered another drink. I looked around the bar. There were five men in the bar and no women. I was back in the American streets.

PITTSBURGH PHIL & CO.

This guy Summerfield was on relief and hitting the wine bottle. He was rather a dull sort, I tried to avoid him, but he was always hanging out the window half-drunk. He'd see me leaving my place and he always said the same thing, "Hey, Hank, how about taking me to the races?" and I always said, "One of these times, Joe, not today." Well, he kept at it, hanging out the window half-drunk, so one day I said, "All right, for Christ's sake, come on . . ." and away we went.

It was January at Santa Anita and if you know that track, it can get real cold out there when you're losing. The wind blows in from the snow on the mountains and your pockets are empty and you shiver and think of death and hard times and no rent and all the rest. It's hardly a pleasant place to lose. At least at Hollywood Park you can come back with a sunburn.

So we went. He talked all the way out. He'd never been to a racetrack. I had to tell him the difference between win, place and show betting. He didn't even know what a starting gate was, or a *Racing Form*. When we got out there he used my *Form*. I had to show him how to read it. I paid his way in and bought him a program. All he had was two dollars. Enough for one bet.

We stood around before the first race looking at the women. Joe told me he hadn't had a woman in five years. He was a shabby-looking guy, a real loser. We passed the *Form* back and forth and looked at the women and then Joe said, "How come the 6 horse is 14 to one? He looks best to me." I tried to explain to Joe why the horse was reading 14 to one in relation to the other horses but he wouldn't listen. "He sure as hell looks best to me. I don't understand. I just gotta bet him." "It's your two dollars, Joe," I said, "and I'm not lending you any money when you lose this one."

The horse's name was Red Charley and he was a sad-looking beast indeed. He came out for the post parade in four bandages. His price leaped to 18 to one when they got a look at him. I put ten win on the logical horse, Bold Latrine, a slight class drop with good earnings and with a live jock and the 2nd leading trainer. I thought that 7 to 2 was a good price on that one.

It was a mile and one sixteenth. Red Charley was reading 20 to one when they came out of the gate and he came out first, you couldn't miss him in all those bandages, and the boy opened up four lengths on the first turn, he must have thought he was in a quarter horse race. The jock only had two wins out of 40 mounts and you could see why. He had six lengths on the backstretch. The lather was running down Red Charley's neck; it damn near looked like shaving cream.

At the top of the turn six lengths had faded to three and the whole pack was gaining on him. At the top of the stretch Red Charley only had a length and a half and my horse Bold Latrine was moving up outside. It looked like I was in. Half way down the stretch I was a neck off. Another lunge and I was in. But they went all the way down to the wire that way. Red Charley still had the neck at the finish. He paid $42.80.

"I thought he looked best," said Joe and he went off to collect his money.

When he came back he asked for the *Form* again. He looked them over. "How come Big H is 6 to one?" he asked me. "He looks best."

"He *may* look best to *you,*" I said, "but off the knowledge of experienced horseplayers and handicappers, real pros, he rates about 6 to one."

"Don't get pissed, Hank. I know I don't know anything about this game. I only mean that to me he looks like he should be the favorite. I gotta bet him anyhow. I might as well go ten win."

"It's your money, Joe. You just lucked it in the first race, the game isn't that easy."

Well Big H won and paid $14.40. Joe started to strut around. We read the *Form* at the bar and he bought us each a drink and tipped the barkeep a buck. As we left the bar he winked at the barkeep and said, "Barney's Mole is all alone in this one." Barney's Mole was the 6/5 favorite so I didn't think that was such a fancy announcement. By the time the race went off Barney's Mole was even money. He paid $4.20 and Joe had $20 win on him.

"That time," he told me, "they made the proper horse the favorite."

Out of the nine races Joe had eight winners. On the ride back he kept wondering how he had missed in the 7th race. "Blue Truck looked far the best. I don't understand how he only got 3rd."

"Joe you had 8 for 9. That's beginner's luck. You don't know how hard this game is."

"It looks easy to me. You just pick the winner and collect your money."

I didn't talk to him the rest of the way in. That night he knocked on my door and he had a fifth of Grandad and the *Racing Form.* I helped him with the bottle while he read the *Form* and told me all nine winners the next day, and why. We had ourselves a real expert here. I know how it can go to a man's head. I had 17 straight winners once and I was going to buy homes along the coast and start a white slavery business to protect my winnings from the income tax man. That's how crazy you can get.

I could hardly wait to take Joe to the track the next day. I wanted to see his face when all his predictions ran out. Horses were only animals made out of flesh. They were fallible. It was like the old horse players said, "There are a dozen ways you can lose a race and only one way to win one."

All right, it didn't happen that way. Joe had 7 for 9—favorites, longshots, medium prices. And he bitched all the way in about his two losers. He couldn't understand it. I didn't talk to him. The son of a bitch could do no wrong. But the percentages would get him. He started telling me how I was betting wrong, and the proper way to bet. Two days at the track and he was an expert. I'd been playing them 20 years and he was telling me I didn't know my ass.

We went all week and Joe kept winning. He got so unbearable I couldn't stand him anymore. He bought a new suit and hat, new shirt and shoes, and started smoking 50 cent cigars. He told the relief people that he was self-employed and didn't need their money anymore. Joe had gone mad. He grew a mustache and purchased a wrist watch and an expensive ring. The next Tuesday I saw him drive to the track in his own car, a '69 black Caddy. He waved to me from his car and flicked out his cigar ash. I didn't talk to him at the track that day. He was in the clubhouse. When he knocked on my door that night he had the usual fifth of Grandad and a tall blonde. A young blonde, well-dressed, well-groomed, she had a shape and a face. They walked in together.

"Who's this old bum?" she asked Joe.

"That's my old buddy, Hank," he told her, "I used to know him when I was poor. He took me to the racetrack one day."

"Don't he have an old lady?"

"Old Hank ain't had a woman since 1965. Listen, how about fixing him up with Big Gertie?"

"Oh hell, Joe, Big Gertie wouldn't go *him!* Look, he's dressed like a rag man."

"Have some mercy, baby, he's my buddy. I know he don't look like much but we both started out together. I'm sentimental."

"Well, Big Gertie ain't sentimental, she likes class."

"Look, Joe," I said, "forget the women. Just sit down with the *Form* and let's have a few drinks and give me some winners for tomorrow."

Joe did that. We drank and he worked them out. He wrote nine horses down for me on a piece of paper. His woman, Big Thelma—well, Big Thelma just looked at me like I was dog shit on somebody's lawn.

Those nine horses were good for eight wins the next day. One horse paid $62.60. I couldn't understand it. That night Joe came by with a new woman. She looked even finer. He sat down with the bottle and the *Form* and wrote me down nine more horses.

Then he told me, "Listen, Hank, I gotta be moving out of my place. I found me a nice deluxe apartment right outside the track. The travel time to and from the track is a nuisance. Let's go, baby. I'll see you around, kid."

I knew that was it. My buddy was giving me the brush-off. The next day I laid it heavy on those nine horses. They were good for seven winners. I went over the *Form* again when I got home trying to figure why he selected the horses he did, but there seemed to be no understandable reason. Some of his selections were truly puzzling to me.

I didn't see Joe again for the remainder of the meet, except once. I saw him walk into the clubhouse with two women. Joe was fat and laughing. He wore a two-hundred-dollar suit and he had a diamond ring on his finger. I lost all nine races that day.

It was two years later. I was at Hollywood Park and it was a particularly hot day, a Thursday, and in the 6th race I happened to land a $26.80 winner. As I was walking away from the payoff window I heard his voice behind me:

"Hey, Hank! *Hank*!"

It was Joe.

"Jesus Christ, man," he said, "it's sure great to see you!"

"Hello Joe . . ."

He still had on his two-hundred-dollar suit in all that heat. The rest of us were in shirt sleeves. He needed a shave and his shoes were scuffed and the suit was wrinkled and dirty. His diamond was gone, his wrist watch was gone.

"Lemme have a smoke, Hank."

I gave him a cigarette and when he lit it I noticed his hands were trembling.

"I need a drink, man," he told me.

I took him over to the bar and we had a couple of whiskeys. Joe studied the *Form*.

"Listen, man, I've put you on plenty of winners, haven't I?"

"Sure, Joe."

We stood there looking at the *Form*. "Now check this race," said Joe. "Look at Black Monkey. He's going to romp, Hank. He's a lock. And at 8 to one."

"You like his chances, Joe?"

"He's in, man. He'll win by daylight."

We placed our bets on Black Monkey and went out to watch the race. He finished a deep 7th.

"I don't understand it," said Joe. "Look, let me have two more bucks, Hank. Siren Call is in the next, she can't lose. There's no way."

Siren Call did get up for 5th but that's not much help when you're betting on the nose. Joe got me for another $2 for the 9th race and his horse ran out there too. Joe told me he didn't have a car and would I mind driving him home?

"You're not going to believe this," he told me, "but I'm back on the dole."

"I believe you, Joe."

"I'll bounce back, though. You know, Pittsburgh Phil went broke half a dozen times. He always sprung back. His friends had faith in him. They lent him money."

When I let him off I found he lived in an old rooming house about four blocks from where I lived. I had never moved. When I let Joe out he said, "There's a hell of a good card tomorrow. You going?"

"I'm not sure, Joe."

"Lemme know if you're going."

"Sure, Joe."

That night I heard the knock on my door. I knew Joe's knock. I didn't answer. I had the T.V. playing but I didn't answer. I just laid real still on the bed. He kept knocking.

"Hank! Hank! You in there? HEY, HANK!"

Then he really beat on the door, the son of a bitch. He seemed frantic. He knocked and he knocked. At last he stopped. I heard him walking down the hall. Then I heard the front door of the apartment house close. I got up, turned off the T.V., went to the refrigerator, made a ham and cheese sandwich, opened a beer. Then I sat down with that, split tomorrow's *Form* open and began looking at the first race, a five-thousand-dollar claimer for colts and geldings three years old and up. I liked the 8 horse. The *Form* had him listed at 5 to one. I'd take that anytime.

DR. NAZI

Now, I'm a man of many problems and I suppose that most of them are self-created. I mean with the female, and gambling, and feeling hostile toward groups of people, and the larger the group, the greater the hostility. I'm called negative and gloomy, sullen.

I keep remembering the female who screamed at me: "You're so god damned negative! Life can be beautiful!"

I suppose it can, and especially with a little less screaming. But I want to tell you about my doctor. I don't go to shrinks. Shrinks are worthless and too contented. But a good doctor is often disgusted and/or mad, and therefore far more entertaining.

I went to Dr. Kiepenheuer's office because it was closest. My hands were breaking out with little white blisters—a sign, I felt, either of my actual anxiety or possible cancer. I wore workingman's gloves so people wouldn't stare. And I burned through the gloves while smoking two packs of cigarettes a day.

I walked into the doctor's place. I had the first appointment. Being a man of anxiety I was thirty minutes early, musing about cancer. I walked across the sitting room and looked into the office. Here was the nurse-receptionist squatted on the floor in her tight white uniform, her dress pulled almost up to her hips, gross and thunderous thighs showing through tightly-pulled nylon. I forgot all about the cancer. She hadn't heard me and I stared at her unveiled legs and thighs, measured the delicious rump with my eyes. She was wiping water from the floor, the toilet had overrun and she was cursing, she was passionate, she was pink and brown and living and unveiled and I stared.

She looked up. "Yes?"

"Go ahead," I said, "don't let me disturb you."

"It's the toilet," she said, "it keeps running over."

She kept wiping and I kept looking over the top of *Life* magazine. She finally stood up. I walked to the couch and sat down. She went through her appointment book.

"Are you Mr. Chinaski?"

"Yes."

"Why don't you take your gloves off? It's warm in here."

"I'd rather not, if you don't mind."

"Dr. Kiepenheuer will be in soon."

"It's all right. I can wait."

"What's your problem?"

"Cancer."

"Cancer?"

"Yes."

The nurse vanished and I read *Life* and then I read another copy of *Life* and then I read *Sports Illustrated* and then I sat staring at paintings of seascapes and landscapes and piped-in music came from somewhere. Then, suddenly, all the lights blinked off, then on again, and I wondered if there would be any way to rape the nurse and get away with it when the doctor walked in. I ignored him and he ignored me, so that went off even.

He called me into his office. He was sitting on a stool and he looked at me. He had a yellow face and yellow hair and his eyes were lusterless. He was dying. He was about 42. I eyed him and gave him six months.

"What's with the gloves?" he asked.

"I'm a sensitive man, Doctor."

"You are?"

"Yes."

"Then I should tell you that I was once a Nazi."

"That's all right."

"You don't mind that I was once a Nazi?"

"No, I don't mind."

"I was captured. They rode us through France in a boxcar with the doors open and the people stood along the way and threw stink bombs and rocks and all sorts of rubbish at us—fishbones, dead plants, excreta, everything imaginable."

Then the doctor sat and told me about his wife. She was trying to skin him. A real bitch. Trying to get all his money. The house. The garden. The garden house. The gardener too, probably, if she hadn't already. And the car. And alimony. Plus a large chunk of cash. Horrible woman. He'd worked so hard. Fifty patients a day at ten dollars a head. Almost impossible to survive. And that woman. Women. Yes, women. He broke down the word for me. I forget if it was woman or female or what it was, but he broke it down into Latin and he broke it down from there to show what the root was—in Latin: women were basically insane.

As he talked about the insanity of women I began to feel pleased with the doctor. My head nodded in agreement.

Suddenly he ordered me to the scales, weighed me, then he listened to my heart and to my chest. He roughly removed my gloves, washed my hands in some kind of shit and opened the blisters with a razor, still talking about the rancor and vengeance that all women carried in their hearts. It was glandular. Women were directed by their glands, men by their hearts. That's why only the men suffered.

He told me to bathe my hands regularly and to throw the god damned gloves away. He talked a little more about women and his wife and then I left.

My next problem was dizzy spells. But I only got them when I was standing in line. I began to get very terrified of standing in line. It was unbearable.

I realized that in America and probably everyplace else it came down to standing in line. We did it everywhere. Driver's license: three or four lines. The racetrack: lines. The movies: lines. The market: lines. I hated lines. I felt there should be a way to avoid them. Then the answer came to me. Have more *clerks*. Yes, that was the answer. Two clerks for every person. *Three* clerks. Let the clerks stand in line.

I knew that lines were killing me. I couldn't accept them, but everybody else did. Everybody else was normal. Life was beautiful for them. They could stand in line without feeling pain. They could stand in line forever. They even *liked* to stand in line. They chatted and grinned and smiled and flirted with each other. They had nothing else to do. They could think of nothing else to do. And I had to look at their ears and mouths and necks and legs and asses and nostrils, all that. I could feel death-rays oozing from their bodies like smog, and listening to their conversations I felt like screaming "*Jesus Christ, somebody help me! Do I have to suffer like this just to buy a pound of hamburger and a loaf of rye bread?"*

The dizziness would come, and I'd spread my legs to keep from falling down; the supermarket would whirl, and the faces of the supermarket clerks with their gold and brown mustaches and their clever happy eyes, all of them going to be supermarket managers someday, with their white scrubbed contented faces, buying homes in Arcadia and nightly mounting their pale blond grateful wives.

I made an appointment with the doctor again. I was given the first appointment. I arrived half an hour early and the toilet was fixed. The nurse was dusting in the office. She bent and straightened and bent halfway and then bent right and then bent left, and she turned her ass toward me and bent over. That white uniform twitched and hiked, climbed, lifted; here was dimpled knee, there was thigh, here was haunch, there was the whole body. I sat down and opened a copy of *Life*.

She stopped dusting and stuck her head out at me, smiling. "You got rid of your gloves, Mr. Chinaski."

"Yes."

The doctor came in looking a bit closer to death and he nodded and I got up and followed him in.

He sat down on his stool.

"Chinaski: how goes it?"

"Well, doctor . . ."

"Trouble with women?"

"Well, of course, but . . ."

He wouldn't let me finish. He had lost more hair. His fingers twitched. He seemed short of breath. Thinner. He was a desperate man.

His wife was skinning him. They'd gone to court. She slapped him in court. He'd liked that. It helped the case. They saw through that bitch. Anyhow, it hadn't come off too badly. She'd left him something. Of course, you know lawyer's fees. Bastards. You ever noticed a lawyer? Almost always fat. Especially around the face. "Anyhow, shit, she nailed me. But I got a little left. You wanna know what a scissors like this costs? Look at it. Tin with a screw. $18.50. My God, and they hated the Nazis. What is a Nazi compared to this?"

"I don't know Doctor. I've told you that I'm a confused man."

"You ever tried a shrink?"

"It's no use. They're dull, no imagination. I don't need the shrinks. I hear they end up sexually molesting their female patients. I'd like to be a shrink if I could fuck all the women; outside of that, their trade is useless."

My doctor hunched up on his stool. He yellowed and greyed a bit more. A giant twitch ran through his body. He was almost through. A nice fellow though.

"Well, I got rid of my wife," he said, "that's over."

"Fine," I said, "tell me about when you were a Nazi."

"Well, we didn't have much choice. They just took us in. I was young. I mean, hell, what are you going to do? You can only live in one country at a time. You go to war, and if you don't end up dead you end up in an open boxcar with people throwing shit at you . . ."

I asked him if he'd fucked his nice nurse. He smiled gently. The smile said yes. Then he told me that since the divorce, well, he'd dated one of his patients, and he knew it wasn't ethical to get that way with patients . . .

"No, I think it's all right, Doctor."

"She's a very intelligent woman. I married her."

"All right."

"Now I'm happy . . . but . . ."

Then he spread his hands apart and opened his palms upward . . .

I told him about my fear of lines. He gave me a standing prescription for Librium.

Then I got a nest of boils on my ass. I was in agony. They tied me with leather straps, these fellows can do anything they want with you, they gave me a local and strapped my ass. I turned my head and looked at my Doctor and said, "Is there any chance of me changing my mind?"

There were three faces looking down at me. His and two others. Him to cut. Her to supply cloths. The third to stick needles.

"You can't change your mind," said the doctor, and he rubbed his hands and grinned and began . . .

The last time I saw him it had something to do with wax in my ears. I could see his lips moving, I tried to understand, but I couldn't hear. I could tell by his eyes and his face that it was hard times for him all over again, and I nodded.

It was warm. I was a bit dizzy and I thought, well, yes, he's a fine fellow but why doesn't he let me tell him about my problems, this isn't fair, I have problems too, and I have to pay him.

Eventually my doctor realized I was deaf. He got something that looked like a fire extinguisher and jammed it into my ears. Later he showed me huge pieces of wax . . . it was the wax, he said. And he pointed down into a bucket. It looked, really, like refried beans.

I got up from the table and paid him and I left. I still couldn't hear anything. I didn't feel particularly bad or good and I wondered what ailment I would bring him next, what he would do about it, what he would do about his 17 year old daughter who was in love with another woman and who was going to marry the woman, and it occurred to me that *everybody* suffered continually, including those who pretended they didn't. It seemed to me that this was quite a discovery. I looked at the newsboy and I thought, hmmmm, hmmmm, and I looked at the next person to pass and I thought hmmmm, hmmmm, hmmmmmm, and at the traffic signal by the hospital a new black car turned the corner and knocked down a pretty young girl in a blue mini dress, and she was blond and had blue ribbons in her hair, and she sat up in the street in the sun and the scarlet ran from her nose.

CHRIST ON ROLLERSKATES

It was a small office on the third floor of an old building not too far from skid row. Joe Mason, president of Rollerworld, Inc., sat behind the worn desk which he rented along with the office. Graffiti were carved on the top and sides: "Born to die." "Some men buy what other men are hanged for." "Shit soup." "I hate love more than I love hate."

The vice president, Clifford Underwood, sat in the only other chair. There was one telephone. The office smelled of urine, but the restroom was 45 feet down the hall. There was a window facing the alley, a thick yellow window that let in a dim light. Both men were smoking cigarettes and waiting.

"When'd you tell 'im?" asked Underwood.

"9:30," said Mason.

"It doesn't matter."

They waited. Eight more minutes. They each lit another cigarette. There was a knock.

"Come in," said Mason. It was Monster Chonjacki, bearded, six foot six and 392 pounds. Chonjacki smelled. It started to rain. You could hear a freightcar going by under the window. It was really 24 freightcars going north filled with commerce. Chonjacki still smelled. He was the star of the Yellowjackets, one of the best roller skaters on either side of the Mississippi, 25 yards to either side.

"Sit down," said Mason.

"No chair," said Chonjacki.

"Make him a chair, Cliff."

The vice president slowly got up, gave every indication of a man about to fart, didn't and walked over and leaned against the rain which beat against the thick yellow window. Chonjacki put both cheeks down, reached and lit up a Pall Mall. No filter. Mason leaned across his desk:

"You are an ignorant son of a bitch."

"Wait a minute, man!"

"You wanna be a hero, don't you sonny? You get excited when little girls without any hair on their pussies scream your name? You like the dear old red, white and blue? Ya like vanilla ice cream? You still beat your tiny little pud, asshole?"

"Listen here, Mason . . ."

"Shut up! Three hundred a week! Three hundred a week I been giving you! When I found you in that bar you didn't have enough for your next drink . . . you had the d.t.'s and were livin' on hogshead soup and cabbage! You couldn't lace on a skate! I made you, asshole, from nothing, and I can make you right back into nothing! As far as you're concerned, I'm God. And I'm a God who doesn't forgive your mother-floppin' sins either!"

Mason closed both eyes and leaned back in the swivel. He inhaled his cigarette; a bit of hot ash dropped on his lower lip but he was too mad to give a damn. He just let the ash burn him. When the ash stopped burning he kept his eyes closed and listened to the rain. Ordinarily he liked to listen to the rain. Especially when he was inside somewhere and the rent was paid and some woman wasn't driving him crazy. But today the rain didn't help. He not only smelled Chonjacki but he felt him there. Chonjacki was worse than diarrhea. Chonjacki was worse than the crabs. Mason opened his eyes, sat up and looked at him. Christ, what a man had to go through just to stay alive.

"Baby," he said softly, "you broke two of Sonny Welborn's ribs last night. You hear me?"

"Listen . . ." Chonjacki started to say.

"Not one rib. No, not just one rib. Two. Two ribs. Hear me?"

"But . . ."

"Listen, asshole! Two ribs! You hear me? Do you hear me?"

"I hear you."

Mason put out his cigarette, got up from the swivel and walked around to Chonjacki's chair. You might say Chonjacki looked nice. You might say he was a handsome kid. You'd never say that about Mason. Mason was old. Forty-nine. Almost bald. Round shouldered. Divorced. Four boys. Two of them in jail. It was still raining. It would rain for almost two days and three nights. The Los Angeles

River would get excited and pretend to be a river.

"Stand up!" said Mason.

Chonjacki stood up. When he did, Mason sunk his left into his gut and when Chonjacki's head came down he put it right back up there with a right chop. Then he felt a little better. It was like a cup of Ovaltine on a coldass morning in January. He walked around and sat down again. This time he didn't light a cigarette. He lit his 15 cent cigar. He lit his after-lunch cigar before lunch. That's how much better he felt. Tension. You couldn't let that shit build. His former brother-in-law had died of a bleeding ulcer. Just because he hadn't known how to let it out.

Chonjacki sat back down. Mason looked at him.

"This, baby, is a *business,* not a sport. We don't believe in *hurting* people, do I get my point across?"

Chonjacki just sat there listening to the rain. He wondered if his car would start. He always had trouble getting his car started when it rained. Otherwise it was a good car.

"I asked you, baby, did I get my point across?"

"Oh, yeah, yeah . . ."

"Two busted ribs. Two of Sonny Welborn's ribs busted. He's our best player."

"Wait! He plays for the Vultures. Welborn plays for the Vultures. How can he be your best player?"

"Asshole! We own the Vultures!"

"You own the Vultures?"

"Yeah, asshole. And the Angels and the Coyotes and the Cannibals and every other damn team in the league, they're all our property, all those boys . . ."

"Jesus . . ."

"No, not Jesus. Jesus doesn't have anything to do with it! But, wait, you give me an idea, asshole."

Mason swiveled toward Underwood who was still leaning against the rain. "It's something to think about," he said.

"Uh," said Underwood.

"Take your head off your pud, Cliff. Think about it."

"About what?"

"Christ on rollerskates. Countless possibilities."

"Yeah. Yeah. We could work in the devil."

"That's good. Yes, the devil."

"We might even work in the cross."

"The cross? No, that's too corny."

Mason swiveled back toward Chonjacki. Chonjacki was still there. He wasn't surprised. If a monkey had been sitting there he wouldn't have been surprised either. Mason had been around too long. But it wasn't a monkey, it was Chonjacki. He had to talk to Chonjacki. Duty, duty . . . all for the rent, an occasional piece of ass and a burial in the country. Dogs had fleas, men had troubles.

"Chonjacki," he said, "please let me explain something to you. Are you listening? Are you capable of listening?"

"I'm listening."

"We're a business. We work five night a week. We're on television. We support families. We pay taxes. We vote. We get tickets from the fucking cops like anybody else. We get toothaches, insomnia, v.d. We've got to live through Christmas and New Year's just like anybody else, you understand?"

"Yes."

"We even, some of us, get depressed sometimes. We're human. I even get depressed. I sometimes feel like crying at night. I sure as hell felt like crying last night when you broke two of Welborn's ribs . . ."

"He was ganging me, Mr. Mason!"

"Chonjacki, Welborn wouldn't pull a hair from your grandmother's left armpit. He reads Socrates, Robert Duncan, and W. H. Auden. He's been in the league five years and he hasn't done enough physical damage to bruise a church-going moth . . ."

"He was coming at me, he was swinging, he was screaming . . ."

"Oh, Christ," said Mason softly. He put his cigar in the ashtray. "Son, I told you. We're a family, a big family. We don't hurt each other. We've got ourselves the finest subnormal audience in sports. We've drawn the biggest breed of idiots alive and they put that money right into our pockets, get it? We've drawn the top-brand idiot right away from professional wrestling, *I Love Lucy*, and George Putnam. We're in, and we don't believe in either malice or violence. Right, Cliff?"

"Right," said Underwood.

"Let's do him a spot," said Mason.

"O.k.," said Underwood.

Mason got up from his desk and moved toward Underwood. "You son of a bitch," he said. "I'll kill you. Your mother swallows her own farts and has a syphilitic urinary tract."

"*Your* mother eats marinated catshit," said Underwood.

He moved away from the window and toward Mason. Mason swung first. Underwood rocked back against the desk.

Mason got a stranglehold around his neck with his left arm and beat Underwood over the head with his right fist and forearm.

"Your sister's tits hang from the bottom of her butt and dangle in the water when she shits," Mason told Underwood. Underwood reached back with one arm and flipped Mason over his head. Mason rolled up against the wall with a crash. Then he got up, walked over to his desk, sat down in the swivel, picked up his cigar and inhaled. It continued to rain. Underwood went back and leaned against the window.

"When a man works five nights a week he can't afford to get injured, understand, Chonjacki?"

"Yes, sir."

"Now look, kid, we got a general rule here—which is . . . Are you listening?"

"Yes."

". . . which is—when anybody in the league injures another player, he's out of a job, he's out of the league, in fact, the word goes out—he's blacklisted at every roller derby in America. Maybe Russia and China and Poland, too. You got that in your head?"

"Yes."

"Now we're letting you get by with this one because we've spent a lot of time and money giving you this buildup. You're the Mark Spitz of our league, but we can bust you just like they can bust him, if you don't do exactly what we tell you."

"Yes, sir."

"But that doesn't mean lay back. You gotta act violent without being violent, get it? The mirror trick, the rabbit out of the hat, the full ton of bologna. They love to be fooled. They don't know the truth, hell they don't even want the truth, it makes them unhappy. We make them happy. We drive new cars and send our kids to college, right?"

"Right."

"O.k., get the hell out of here."

Chonjacki rose to leave.

"And kid . . ."

"Yes?"

"Take a bath once in awhile."
"What?"
"Well, maybe that isn't it. Do you use enough toilet paper when you wipe your ass?"
"I don't know. How much is enough?"
"Didn't your mother tell you?"
"What?"
"You keep wiping until you can't see it anymore."
Chonjacki just stood there looking at him.
"All right, you can go now. And please remember everything I've told you."
Chonjacki left. Underwood walked over and sat down in the vacant chair. He took out his after-lunch 15 cent cigar and lit it. The two men sat there for five minutes without saying anything. Then the phone rang. Mason picked it up. He listened, then said, "Oh, Boy Scout Troop 763? How many? Sure, sure, we'll let 'em in for half price. Sunday night. We'll rope off a section. Sure, sure. Oh, it's all right . . ." He hung up.
"Assholes," he said.
Underwood didn't answer. They sat listening to the rain. The smoke from their cigars made interesting designs in the air. They sat and smoked and listened to the rain and watched the designs in the air. The phone rang again and Mason made a face. Underwood got up from his chair, walked over and answered it. It was his turn.

A SHIPPING CLERK WITH A RED NOSE

When I first met Randall Harris he was 42 and lived with a grey haired woman, one Margie Thompson. Margie was 45 and not too handsome. I was editing the little magazine *Mad Fly* at the time and I had come over in an attempt to get some material from Randall.

Randall was known as an isolationist, a drunk, a crude and bitter man but his poems were raw, raw and honest, simple and savage. He was writing unlike anybody else at the time. He worked as a shipping clerk in an auto parts warehouse.

I sat across from both Randall and Margie. It was 7:15 p.m. and Harris was already drunk on beer. He set a bottle in front of me. I'd heard of Margie Thompson. She was an old-time communist, a world-saver, a do-gooder. One wondered what she was doing with Randall who cared for nothing and admitted it. "I like to photograph shit," he told me, "that's my art."

Randall had begun writing at the age of 38. At 42, after three small chapbooks (*Death Is a Dirtier Dog Than My Country*, *My Mother Fucked an Angel*, and *The Piss-Wild Horses of Madness*), he was getting what might be called critical acclaim. But he made nothing on his writing and he said, "I'm nothing but a shipping clerk with the deep blue blues." He lived in an old front court in Hollywood with Margie, and he was weird, truly. "I just don't like people," he said. "You know, Will Rogers once said, 'I never met a man I didn't like.' Me, I never met a man I liked."

But Randall had humor, an ability to laugh at pain and at himself. You liked him. He was an ugly man with a large head and a smashed-up face—only the nose seemed to have escaped the general smashup. "I don't have enough bone in my nose, it's like rubber," he explained. His nose was long and very red.

I had heard stories about Randall. He was given to smashing windows and breaking bottles against the wall. He was one nasty drunk. He also had periods where he wouldn't answer the door or the telephone. He didn't own a T.V., only a small radio and he only listened to symphony music—strange for a guy as crude as he was.

Randall also had periods when he took the bottom off the telephone and stuffed toilet paper around the bell so it wouldn't ring. It stayed that way for months. One wondered why he had a phone. His education was sparse but he'd evidently read most of the best writers.

"Well, fucker," he said to me, "I guess you wonder what I'm doing with her?" he pointed to Margie.

I didn't answer.

"She's a good lay," he said, "and she gives me some of the best sex west of St. Louis."

This was the same guy who had written four or five great love poems to a woman called Annie. You wondered how it worked.

Margie just sat there and grinned. She wrote poetry too but it wasn't very good. She attended two workshops a week which hardly helped.

"So you want some poems?" he asked me.

"Yes, I'd like to look some over."

Harris walked over to the closet, opened the door and picked some torn and crushed papers off the floor. He handed them to me. "I wrote these last night." Then he walked into the kitchen and came out with two more beers. Margie didn't drink.

I began to read the poems. They were all powerful. He typed with a very heavy hand and the words seemed chiseled in the paper. The force of his writing always astounded me. He seemed to be saying all the things we should have said but had never thought of saying.

"I'll take these poems," I said.

"O.k.," he said. "Drink up."

When you came to see Harris, drinking was a must. He smoked one cigarette after another. He dressed in loose brown chino pants two sizes too large and old shirts that were always ripped. He was around six feet and 220 pounds, much of it beerfat. He was round-shouldered, and peered out at you from behind slitted eyelids. We drank a good two hours and a half, the room heavy with smoke.

Suddenly Harris stood up and said, "Get the hell out of here, fucker, you disgust me!"

"Easy now, Harris . . ."

"I said NOW!, fucker!"

I got up and left with the poems.

I returned to that front court two months later to deliver a couple of copies of *Mad Fly* to Harris. I had run all ten of his poems. Margie let me in. Randall wasn't there.

"He's in New Orleans," said Margie, "I think he's getting a break. Jack Teller wants to publish his next book but he wants to meet Randall first. Teller says he can't print anybody he doesn't like. He's paid the air fare both ways."

"Randall isn't exactly endearing," I said.

"We'll see," said Margie. "Teller's a drunk and an ex-con. They might make a lovely pair."

Teller put out the magazine *Rifraff* and had his own press. He did very fine work. The last issue of *Rifraff* had had Harris' ugly face on the cover sucking at a beer-bottle and had featured a number of his poems.

Rifraff was generally recognized as the number one lit mag of the time. Harris was beginning to get more and more notice. This would be a good chance for him if he didn't botch it with his mean tongue and his drunken manners. Before I left Margie told me she was pregnant—by Harris. As I said, she was 45.

"What'd he say when you told him?"

"He seemed indifferent."

I left.

The book did come out in an edition of 2,000, finely printed. The cover was made of cork imported from Ireland. The pages were vari-colored, of extremely good paper, set in rare type and interspersed with some of Harris' India ink sketches. The book received acclaim, both for itself and its contents. But Teller couldn't pay royalties. He and his wife lived on a very narrow margin. In ten years the book would go for $75 on the rare book market. Meanwhile Harris went back to his shipping clerk job at the auto parts warehouse.

When I called again four or five months later Margie was gone.

"She's been gone a long time," said Harris. "Have a beer."

"What happened?"

"Well, after I got back from New Orleans, I wrote a few short stories. While I was at work she got to poking around in my drawers. She read a couple of my stories and took exception to them."

"What were they about?"

"Oh, she read something about my climbing in and out of bed with some women in New Orleans."

"Were the stories true?" I asked.

"How's *Mad Fly* doing?" he asked.

The baby was born, a girl, Naomi Louise Harris. She and her mother lived in Santa Monica and Harris drove out once a week to see them. He paid child support and continued to drink his beer. Next I knew he had a weekly column in the underground newspaper *L.A. Lifeline.* He called his colums *Sketches of a First Class Maniac.* His prose was like his poetry—undisciplined, antisocial, and lazy.

Harris grew a goatee and grew his hair longer. The next time I saw him he was living with a 35-year-old girl, a pretty redhead called Susan. Susan worked in an art supply store, painted, and played fair guitar. She also drank an occasional beer with Randall which was more than Margie had done. The court seemed cleaner. When Harris finished a bottle he threw it into a paper bag instead of throwing it on the floor. He was still a nasty drunk, though.

"I'm writing a novel," he told me, "and I'm getting a poetry reading now and then at nearby universities. I also have one coming up in Michigan and one in New Mexico. The offers are pretty good. I don't like to read, but I'm a good reader. I give them a show and I give them some good poetry."

Harris was also beginning to paint. He didn't paint very well. He painted like a five-year-old drunk on vodka but he managed to sell one or two for $40 or $50. He told me that he was considering quitting his job. Three weeks later he did quit in order to make the Michigan reading. He'd already used his vacation for the New Orleans trip.

I remember once he had vowed to me, "I'll never read in front of those bloodsuckers, Chinaski. I'll go to my grave without ever giving a poetry reading. It's vanity, it's a sell-out." I didn't remind him of his statement.

His novel *Death in the Life of All the Eyes On Earth* was brought out by a small but prestige press which paid standard royalties. The reviews were good, including one in *The New York Review of Books*. But he was still a nasty drunk and had many fights with Susan over his drinking.

Finally, after one horrible drunk, when he had raved and cursed and screamed all night, Susan left him. I saw Randall several days after her departure. Harris was strangely quiet, hardly nasty at all.

"I loved her, Chinaski," he told me. "I'm not going to make it, baby."

"You'll make it, Randall. You'll see. You'll make it. The human being is much more durable than you think."

"Shit," he said. "I hope you're right. I've got this damned hole in my gut. Women have put many a good man under the bridge. They don't feel it like we do."

"They feel it. She just couldn't handle your drinking."

"Fuck, man, I write most of my stuff when I'm drunk."

"Is that the secret?"

"Shit, yes. Sober, I'm just a shipping clerk and not a very good one at that . . ."

I left him there hanging over his beer.

I made the rounds again three months later. Harris was still in his front court. He introduced me to Sandra, a nice-looking blonde of 27. Her father was a superior court judge and she was a graduate of U.S.C. Besides being well-shaped she had a cool sophistication that had been lacking in Randall's other women. They were drinking a bottle of good Italian wine.

Randall's goatee had turned into a beard and his hair was much longer. His clothes were new and in the latest style. He had on $40 shoes, a new wristwatch and his face seemed thinner, his fingernails clean . . . but his nose still reddened as he drank the wine.

"Randall and I are moving to West L.A. this weekend," she told me. "This place is filthy."

"I've done a lot of good writing here," he said.

"Randall, dear," she said, "it isn't the *place* that does the writing, it's *you*. I think we might get Randall a job teaching three days a week."

"I can't teach."

"Darling, you can teach them *everything*."

"Shit," he said.

"They're thinking of doing a movie of Randall's book. We've seen the script. It's a very fine script."

"A movie?" I asked.

"There's not much chance," said Harris.

"Darling, it's in the works. Have a little faith."

I had another glass of wine with them, then left. Sandra was a beautiful girl.

I wasn't given Randall's West L.A. address and didn't make any attempt to find him. It was over a year later when I read the review of the movie *Flower Up the Tail of Hell.* It had been taken from his novel. It was a fine review and Harris even had an acting bit in the film.

I went to see it. They'd done a good job on the book. Harris looked a little more austere than when I had last seen him. I decided to find him. After a bit of detective work I knocked on the door of his cabin in Malibu one night about 9:00 p.m. Randall answered the door.

"Chinaski, you old dog," he said. "Come on in."

A beautiful girl sat on the couch. She appeared to be about 19, she simply radiated natural beauty. "This is Karilla," he said. They were drinking a bottle of expensive French wine. I sat down with them and had a glass. I had several glasses. Another bottle came out and we talked quietly. Harris didn't get drunk and nasty and didn't appear to smoke as much.

"I'm working on a play for Broadway," he told me. "They say the theatre is dying but I have something for them. One of the leading producers is interested. I'm getting the last act in shape now. It's a good medium. I was always splendid on conversation, you know."

"Yes," I said.

I left about 11:30 that night. The conversation had been pleasant . . . Harris had begun to show a distinguished grey about the temples and he didn't say "shit" more than four or five times.

The play *Shoot Your Father, Shoot Your God, Shoot Away the Disentanglement* was a success. It had one of the longest runs in Broadway history. It had everything: something for the revolutionaries, something for the reactionaries, something for lovers of comedy, something for lovers of drama, even something for the intellectuals, and it still made sense. Randall Harris moved from Malibu to a large place high in the Hollywood Hills. You read about him now in the syndicated gossip columns.

I went to work and found the location of his Hollywood Hills place, a three-story mansion which overlooked the lights of Los Angeles and Hollywood.

I parked, got out of the car, and walked up the path to the front door. It was around 8:30 p.m., cool, almost cold; there was a full moon and the air was fresh and clear.

I rang the bell. It seemed a very long wait. Finally the door opened. It was the butler. "Yes, sir?" he asked me.

"Henry Chinaski to see Randall Harris," I said.

"Just a moment, sir." He closed the door quietly and I waited. Again a long time. Then the butler was back. "I'm sorry, sir, but Mr. Harris can't be disturbed at this time."

"Oh, all right."

"Would you care to leave a message, sir?"

"A message?"

"Yes, a message."

"Yes, tell him 'congratulations.' "

" 'Congratulations?' Is that all?"

"Yes, that's all."

"Goodnight, sir."

"Goodnight."

I went back to my car, got in. It started and I began the long drive down out of the hills. I had that early copy of *Mad Fly* with me that I had wanted him to sign. It was the copy with ten of Randall Harris' poems in it. He probably was busy. Maybe, I thought, if I mail the magazine to him with a stamped return envelope, he'll sign.

It was only about 9:00 p.m. There was time for me to go somewhere else.

THE DEVIL WAS HOT

Well, it was after an argument with Flo and I didn't feel like getting drunk or going to a massage parlor. So I got in my car and drove west toward the beach. It was along toward evening and I drove slowly. I got to the pier, parked, and walked on up the pier. I stopped in the penny arcade, played a few games, but the place stank of piss so I walked out. I was too old to ride the merry-go-round so I passed that. The usual types walked the pier—a sleepy indifferent crowd.

It was then I noticed a roaring sound coming from a nearby building. A tape or record, no doubt. There was a barker out front: "Yes, ladies and gentlemen, *Inside, Inside here* . . . we actually have captured the *devil*! He is on display to see with your own eyes! Think, just for a quarter, twenty-five cents, you can actually *see* the devil . . . the biggest loser of all time! The loser of the only revolution ever attempted in Heaven!"

Well, I was ready for a little comedy to offset what Flo was putting me through. I paid my quarter and stepped inside with six or seven other assorted suckers. They had this guy in a cage. They'd sprayed him red and he had something in his mouth that made him puff out little rolls of smoke and spurts of flame. He wasn't putting on a very good show. He was just walking around in circles, saying over and over again, "God damn it, I've got to get *out* of here! How'd I ever get in this friggin' fix?" Well, I'll tell you he *did* look dangerous. Suddenly he did six rapid back flips. On his last flip he landed on his feet, looked around and said, "Oh shit, I feel awful!"

Then he saw me. He walked right over to where I was standing next to the wire. He was warm like a heater. I don't know how they worked that.

"My son," he said, "you've come at last! I've been waiting. Thirty-two days I've been in this fucking cage!"

"I don't know what you're talking about."

"My son," he said, "don't joke with me. Come back late tonight with the wire-cutters and free me."

"Don't lay any shit on me, man," I said

"Thirty-two days I've been in here, my son! At last I have my freedom!"

"You mean you claim you're really the devil?"

"I'll screw a cat's ass if I'm not," he answered.

"If you're the devil then you can use your supernatural powers to get out of here."

"My powers have temporarily vanished. This guy, the barker, he was in the drunk tank with me. I told him I was the devil and he bailed me out. I'd lost my powers in that jail or I wouldn't have needed him. He got me drunk again and when I woke up I was in this cage. The cheap bastard, he feeds me dogfood and peanut butter sandwiches. My son, help me, I beg you!"

"You're crazy," I said, "you're some kind of nut."

"Just come back tonight, my son, with the wire-clippers."

The barker walked in and announced that the session with the devil was over and if we wanted to see him anymore it'd be another twenty-five cents. I'd seen enough. I walked out with the six or seven other assorted suckers.

"Hey, he *talked* to you," said a little old guy walking next to me, "I've seen him every night and you're the first person he has ever talked to."

"Balls," I said.

The barker stopped me. "What'd he tell you? I saw him talking to you. What'd he tell you?"

"He told me everything," I said.

"Well, hands off, buddy, he's *mine!* I ain't made so much money since I had the bearded three-legged lady."

"What happened to her?"

"She ran away with the octopus man. They're running a farm in Kansas."

"I think you people are all crazy."

"I'm just telling you, I found this guy. *Keep off!*"

I walked to my car, got in and drove back to Flo. When I got there she was sitting in the kitchen drinking whiskey. She sat there and told me a few hundred times what a useless hunk of man I was. I drank with her a while not saying much myself. Then I got up, went to the garage, got the wire-cutters, put them in my pocket, got in the car and drove back to the pier.

I broke in the back way, the latch was rusty and snapped right off. He was asleep on the floor of the cage. I began trying to cut the wire but I couldn't cut through it. The wire was very thick. Then he woke up.

"My son," he said, "you came back! I knew you would!"

"Look, man, I can't cut the wire with these clippers. The wire's too thick."

He stood up. "Hand 'em here."

"God," I said, "your hands are hot! You must have some kind of fever."

"Don't call me God," he said.

He snipped the wire with the clippers like it was thread and stepped out. "And now, my son, to your place. I've got to get my strength back. A few porterhouse steaks and I'll be straight. I've eaten so much dogfood I'm afraid I'm going to bark any minute."

We walked back to my car and I drove him to my place. When we walked in Flo was still sitting in the kitchen drinking whiskey. I fried him a bacon and egg sandwich for starters and we sat down with Flo.

"Your friend is a handsome looking devil," she told me.

"He claims to *be* the devil," I said.

"Been a long time," he said, "since I had me a hunk of good woman."

He leaned over and gave Flo a long kiss. When he let go she seemed to be in a state of shock. "That was the *hottest* kiss I *ever* had," she said, "and I've had plenty."

"Really?" he asked.

"If you make love anything like the way you kiss, it would simply be too much, just simply too *much*!"

"Where's your bedroom?" he asked me.

"Just follow the lady," I said.

He followed Flo to the bedroom and I poured a deep whiskey.

I never heard such screams and moans and it went on for a good forty-five minutes. Then he walked out alone and sat down and poured himself a drink.

"My son," he said, "you got yourself a good woman there."

He walked to the couch in the front room, stretched out and fell asleep. I walked into the bedroom, undressed, and climbed in with Flo.

"My god," she said, "my god, I don't believe it. He put me through heaven and hell."

"I just hope he doesn't set the couch on fire," I said.

"You mean he smokes cigarettes and falls asleep?"

"Forget it," I said.

Well, he began taking over. *I* had to sleep on the couch. I had to listen to Flo screaming and moaning in there every night. One day while Flo was at the market and we were having a beer in the breakfast nook I had a talk with him. "Listen," I said, "I don't mind helping somebody out, but now I've lost my bed and my wife. I'm going to have to ask you to leave."

"I believe I'll stay a while, my son, your old lady is one of the best pieces I've ever had."

"Listen, man," I said, "I might have to take extreme means to remove you."

"Tough boy, eh? Well look tough boy, I got a little news for you. My supernatural powers have returned. If you try to fuck with me you might get burned. Watch!"

We've got a dog. Old Bones; he's not worth much but he barks at night, he's a fair watchdog. Well, he pointed his finger at Old Bones, the finger kind of made a sneezing sound, then it sizzled and a thin line of flame ran up and touched Old Bones. Old Bones frizzled-up and vanished. He just wasn't there anymore. No bone, no fur, not even any stink. Just space.

"O.k., man," I told him. "You can stay a couple of days but after that you gotta leave."

"Fry me up a porterhouse," he said, "I'm hungry, and I'm afraid my sperm-count is dropping off."

I got up and threw a steak in the pan.

"Cook me up some french fries to go with that," he said, "and some sliced tomato. I don't need any coffee. Been having insomnia. I'll just have a couple more beers."

By the time I got the food in front of him, Flo was back.

"Hello, my love," she said, "how you doing?"

"Just fine," he said, "don't you have any catsup?"
I walked out, got in my car and drove down to the beach.

Well, the barker had another devil in there. I paid my quarter and went in. This devil really wasn't much. The red paint sprayed on him was killing him and he was drinking to keep from going crazy. He was a big guy but he didn't have any qualities at all. I was one of the few customers in there. There were more flies in there than there were people.

The barker walked up to me. "I'm starving to death since you stole the real thing from me. I suppose you got a show of your own going?"

"Listen," I said, "I'd give anything to give him back to you. I was just trying to be a good guy."

"You know what happens to good guys in this world, don't you?"

"Yeah, they end up standing down at 7th and Broadway selling copies of the *Watchtower.*"

"My name's Ernie Jamestown," he said, "tell me all about it. We got a room in the back."

I walked to the room in the back with Ernie. His wife was sitting at the table drinking whiskey. She looked up.

"Listen, Ernie, if this bastard is gonna be our new devil, forget it. We might just as well stage a triple suicide."

"Take it easy," said Ernie, "and pass the bottle."

I told Ernie everything that had happened. He listened carefully and then said, "I can take him off your hands. He has two weaknesses—drink and women. And there's one other thing. I don't know why it happens but when he's confined, like he was in the drunk tank or in that cage out there, he loses his supernatural powers. All right, we take it from there."

Ernie went to the closet and dragged out a mass of chains and padlocks. Then he went to the phone and asked for an Edna Hemlock. Edna Hemlock was to meet us in twenty minutes at the corner outside Woody's Bar. Ernie and I got in my car, stopped for two fifths at the liquor store, met Edna, picked her up, and drove to my place.

They were still in the kitchen. They were necking like mad. But as soon as he saw Edna the devil forgot all about my old lady. He dropped her like a pair of stained panties. Edna had it all. They'd made no mistakes when they put her together.

"Why don't you two drink up and get acquainted?" said Ernie. Ernie put a large glass of whiskey in front of each of them.

The devil looked at Ernie. "Hey, mother, you're the guy who put me in that cage, ain't ya?"

"Forget it," said Ernie, "let's let bygones be bygones."

"Like hell!" He pointed a finger and the line of flame ran up to Ernie and he was no longer there.

Edna smiled and lifted her whiskey. The devil grinned, lifted his and gulped it down.

"Fine stuff!" he said. "Who bought it?"

"That man who just left the room a moment ago," I said.

"Oh."

He and Edna had another drink and began eyeballing each other. Then my old lady spoke to him:

"Take your eyes off that tramp!"

"What tramp?"

"Her!"

"Just drink your drink and shut up!"

He pointed his finger at my old lady, there was a small crackling sound and she was gone. Then he looked at me:

"And what have you got to say?"

"Oh, I'm the guy who brought the wire-cutters, remember? I'm here to run little errands, bring in towels, so forth . . ."

"It sure feels good to have my supernatural powers again."

"They do come in handy," I said, "we got an overpopulation problem anyhow."

He was eyeballing Edna. Their eyes were so locked that I was able to lift one of the fifths of whiskey. I took the fifth and got in my car with it and drove back to the beach again.

Ernie's wife was still sitting in the back room. She was glad to see the new fifth and I poured two drinks.

"Who's the kid you got locked in the cage?" I asked.

"Oh, he's a third-string quarterback from one of the local colleges. He's trying to pick up a little spare change."

"You sure have nice breasts," I said.

"You think so? Ernie never says anything about my breasts."

"Drink up. This is good stuff."

I slid over next to her. She had nice fat thighs. When I kissed her, she didn't resist.

"I get so tired of this life," she said, "Ernie's always been a cheap hustler. You got a good job?"

"Oh yeah. I'm head shipping clerk at Drombo-Western."

"Kiss me again," she said.

I rolled off and wiped myself with the sheet.

"If Ernie finds out he'll kill us both," she said.

"Ernie isn't going to find out. Don't worry about it."

"You make great love," she said, "but why *me*?"

"I don't understand."

"I mean, really, what made you do it?"

"Oh, I said, "the devil made me do it."

Then I lit a cigarette, laid back, inhaled, and blew a perfect smoke ring. She got up and went to the bathroom. In a minute I heard the toilet flush.

GUTS

Like anybody can tell you, I am not a very nice man. I don't know the word. I have always admired the villain, the outlaw, the son of a bitch. I don't like the clean-shaven boy with the necktie and the good job. I like desperate men, men with broken teeth and broken minds and broken ways. They interest me. They are full of surprises and explosions. I also like vile women, drunk cursing bitches with loose stockings and sloppy mascara faces. I'm more interested in perverts than saints. I can relax with bums because I am a bum. I don't like laws, morals, religions, rules. I don't like to be shaped by society.

I was drinking with Marty, the ex-con, up in my room one night. I didn't have a job. I didn't want a job. I just wanted to sit around with my shoes off and drink wine and talk, and laugh if possible. Marty was a little dull, but he had workingman's hands, a broken nose, mole's eyes, nothing much to him but he'd been through it.

"I like you, Hank," said Marty, "you're a real man, you're one of the few real men I've known."

"Yeh," I said.

"You got guts."

"Yeh."

"I was a hard-rock miner once . . ."

"Yeh?"

"I got in a fight with this guy. We used ax handles. He broke my left arm with his first swing. I went on to fight him. I beat his god-damned head in. When he came around from that beating, he was out of his head. I'd mashed his brains in. They put him in a mad-house."

"That's all right," I said.

"Listen," said Marty, "I want to fight you."

"You get first punch. Go ahead, hit me."

Marty was sitting in a straight-backed green chair. I was walking to the sink to pour another glass of wine from the bottle. I turned around and smashed him a right to the face. He flipped over backwards in the chair, got up and came toward me. I wasn't looking for the left. It got me high on the forehead and knocked me down. I reached into a paper sack full of vomit and empties, came out with a bottle, rose to my knees and hurled it. Marty ducked and I came up with the chair behind me. I had it over my head when the door opened. It was our landlady, a good-looking young blonde in her twenties. What she was doing running a place like that I could never figure out. I put the chair down.

"Go to your room, Marty."

Marty looked ashamed, like a little boy. He walked down the hall to his room, walked in and closed the door.

"Mr. Chinaski," she said, "I want you to know . . ."

"I want you to know," I said, "that it's no use."

"What's no use?"

"You're not my type. I don't want to fuck you."

"Listen," she said, "I want to tell you something. I saw you pissing in the lot next door last night and if you do that again I'm going to throw you out of here. Somebody's been pissing in the elevator too. Has that been you?"

"I don't piss in elevators."

"Well, I saw you in the lot last night. I was watching. It was you."

"The hell it was me."

"You were too drunk to know. Don't do it again."

She closed the door and was gone.

I was sitting there quietly drinking wine a few minutes later and trying to remember if I *had* pissed in the lot, when there was a knock on the door.

"Come in," I said.

It was Marty. "I gotta tell you something."

"Sure. Sit down."

I poured Marty a glass of port and he sat down.

"I'm in love," he said.

I didn't answer. I rolled a cigarette.

"You believe in love?" he asked.
"I have to. It happened to me once."
"Where is she?"
"She's gone. Dead."
"Dead? How?"
"Drink."
"This one drinks too. It worries me. She's always drunk. She can't stop."
"None of us can."
"I go to A.A. meetings with her. She's drunk when she goes. Half of them down there at the A.A. are drunk. You can smell the fumes."
I didn't answer.
"God, she's young. And what a body! I love her, man, really love her!"
"Oh hell, Marty, that's just sex."
"No, I love her, Hank, I really feel it."
"I guess it's possible."
"Christ, they've got her down in a cellar room. She can't pay her rent."
"The cellar?"
"Yeah, they got a room down there with all the boilers and shit."
"Hard to believe."
"Yeah, she's down there. And I love her, man, and I don't have any money to help her with."
"That's sad. I been in the same situation. It hurts."
"If I can get straight, if I can get on the wagon for ten days and get my health back—I can get a job somewhere, I can help her."
"Well," I said, "you're drinking now. If you love her, you'll stop drinking. Right now."
"By god," he said, "I will! I'll pour this drink into the sink!"
"Don't be melodramatic. Just pass that glass over here."

I took the elevator down to the first floor with the fifth of cheap whiskey I had stolen at Sam's liquor store a week earlier. Then I took the stairway to the cellar. There was a small light burning down there. I walked along looking for a door. I finally found one. It must have been 1:00 or 2:00 in the morning. I knocked. The door opened a notch and here stood a really fine-looking woman in a negligee. I hadn't expected that. Young, and a strawberry blonde.

I stuck my foot in the door, then I pushed my way in, closed the door and looked around. Not a bad place at all.

"Who are you?" she asked. "Get out of here."

"This is a nice place you got here. I like it better than my own."

"Get out of here! Get out! Get out!"

I pulled the fifth of whiskey out of the paper bag. She looked at it.

"What's your name?" I asked.

"Jeanie."

"Look, Jeanie, where do you keep your drinking glasses?"

She pointed to a wall shelf and I walked over and got two tall water glasses. There was a sink. I put a little water in each, then walked over, set them down, opened the whiskey and mixed it in. We sat on the edge of her bed and drank. She was young, attractive. I couldn't believe it. I waited for a neurotic explosion, for something psychotic. Jeanie looked normal, even healthy. But she did like her whiskey. She drank right along with me. Having come down there in a rush of eagerness, I no longer felt that eagerness. I mean, if she had had a little pig in her or something indecent or foul (a harelip, anything), I would have felt more like moving in. I remembered a story I had read in the *Racing Form* once about a high-bred stallion they couldn't get to mate with the mares. They got the most beautiful mares they could find, but the stallion only shied away. Then somebody, who knew something, got an idea. He smeared mud all over a beautiful mare and the stallion immediately mounted her. The theory was that the stallion felt inferior to all the beauty and when it was muddied-up, fouled, he at least felt equal or maybe even superior. Horses' minds and men's minds could be a great deal alike.

Anyhow, Jeanie poured the next drink and asked me my name and where I roomed. I told her that I was upstairs somewhere and I just wanted to drink with somebody.

"I saw you at the Clamber-In one night about a week ago," she said, "you were very funny, you had everybody laughing, you bought everybody drinks."

"I don't remember."

"I remember. You like my negligee?"

"Yes."

"Why don't you take off your pants and get more comfortable?"

I did and sat back on the bed with her. It moved very slowly. I remember telling her that she had nice breasts and then I was sucking on one of them. Next I knew we were at it. I was on top. But something didn't work. I rolled off.

"I'm sorry," I said.

"It's all right," she said, "I still like you."

We sat there talking vaguely and finishing the whiskey.

Then she got up and turned off the lights. I felt very sad and climbed into bed and lay against her back. Jeanie was warm, full, and I could feel her breathing, and I could feel her hair against my face. My penis begain to rise and I poked it against her. I felt her reach down and guide it in.

"Now," she said, "now, that's it . . ."

It was good that way, long and good, and then we were finished and then we slept.

When I woke up she was still asleep and I got up to get dressed. I was fully clothed when she turned and looked at me: "One more time before you go."

"All right."

I undressed again and got in with her. She turned her back to me and we did it again, the same way. After I climaxed she lay with her back to me.

"Will you come see me again?" she asked.

"Of course."

"You live upstairs?"

"Yes. 309. I can come see you or you can come see me."

"I'd rather you came to see me," she said.

"All right," I said. I got dressed, opened the door, closed the door, walked up the stairway, got in the elevator, and hit the 3 button.

It was about a week later, one night, I was drinking wine with Marty. We talked about various things of no importance and then he said, "Christ, I feel awful."

"What again?"

"Yeah. My girl, Jeanie. I told you about her."

"Yes. The one who lives in the cellar. You're in love with her."

"Yeh. They kicked her out of the cellar. She couldn't even make the cellar rent."

"Where'd she go?"

"I don't know. She's gone. I heard they kicked her out. Nobody knows what she did, where she went. I went to the A.A. meeting. She wasn't there. I'm sick, Hank, I'm really sick. I loved her. I'm about out of my head."

I didn't answer.

"What can I do, man? I'm really torn apart . . ."

"Let's drink to her luck, Marty, to her good luck."

We had a good long one to her.

"She was all right, Hank, you gotta believe me, she was all right."

"I believe you Marty."

A week later Marty got kicked out for not paying his rent and I got a job in a meat packing plant and there were a couple of Mexican bars across the street. I liked those Mexican bars. After work, I smelled of blood, but nobody seemed to mind. It wasn't until I got on the bus to go back to my room that those noses started raising and I got the dirty looks, and I began feeling mean again. That helped.

HIT MAN

Ronnie was to meet the two men at the German bar in the Silverlake district. It was 7:15 p.m. He sat there drinking the dark beer at the table by himself. The barmaid was blond, fine ass, and her breasts looked as if they were going to fall out of her blouse.

Ronnie liked blondes. It was like iceskating and rollerskating. The blondes were iceskating, the rest were rollerskating. The blondes even smelled different. But women meant trouble, and for him the trouble often outweighed the joy. In other words, the price was too high.

Yet a man needed a woman now and then, if for no other reason than to prove he could get one. The sex was secondary. It wasn't a lover's world, it never would be.

7:20. He waved her over for another beer. She came smiling, carrying the beer out in front of her breasts. You couldn't help liking her like that.

"You like working here?" he asked her.

"Oh yes, I meet a lot of men."

"Nice men?"

"Nice men and the other kind."

"How can you tell them apart?"

"I can tell by looking."

"What kind of man am I?"

"Oh," she laughed, "nice, of course."

"You've earned your tip," said Ronnie.

7:25. They'd said 7. Then he looked up. It was Curt. Curt had the guy with him. They came over and sat down. Curt waved for a pitcher.

"The Rams ain't worth shit," said Curt, "I've lost an even $500

on them this season."
"You think Prothro's finished?"
"Yeah, it's over for him," said Curt. "Oh, this is Bill. Bill, this is Ronnie."
They shook hands. The barmaid arrived with the pitcher.
"Gentlemen," said Ronnie, "this is Kathy."
"Oh," said Bill.
"Oh, yes," said Curt.
The barmaid laughed and wiggled off.
"It's good beer," said Ronnie. "I've been here since 7:00, waiting. I ought to know."
"You don't want to get drunk," said Curt.
"Is he reliable?" asked Bill.
"He's got the best references," said Curt.
"Look," said Bill, "I don't want comedy. It's my money."
"How do I know you're not a pig?" asked Ronnie.
"How do I know you won't cut with the $2500?"
"Three grand."
"Curt said two and one half."
"I just upped it. I don't like you."
"I don't care too much for your ass either. I've got a good mind to call it off."
"You won't. You guys never do."
"Do you do this regular?"
"Yes. Do you?"
"All right, gentlemen," said Curt, "I don't care what you settle for. I get my grand for the contract."
"You're the lucky one, Curt," said Bill.
"Yeah," said Ronnie.
"Each man is an expert in his own line," said Curt, lighting a cigarette.
"Curt, how do I know this guy won't cut with the three grand?"
"He won't or he's out of business. It's the only kind of work he can do."
"That's horrible," said Bill.
"What's horrible about it? You need him don't you?"
"Well, yes."
"Other people need him too. They say each man is good at something. He's good at that."
Somebody put some money in the juke and they sat listening to

the music and drinking the beer.

"I'd really like to give it to that blonde," said Ronnie. "I'd like to give her about six hours of turkeyneck."

"I would too," said Curt, "if I had it."

"Let's get another pitcher," said Bill. "I'm nervous.

"There's nothing to worry about," said Curt. He waved for another pitcher of beer. "That $500 I dropped on the Rams, I'll get it back at Anita. They open December 26th. I'll be there."

"Is the Shoe going to ride in the meet?" asked Bill.

"I haven't read the papers. I'd imagine he will. He can't quit. It's in his blood."

"Longden quit," said Ronnie.

"Well, he had to; they had to strap the old man in the saddle."

"He won his last race."

"Campus pulled the other horse."

"I don't think you can beat the horses," said Bill.

"A smart man can beat anything he puts his mind to," said Curt. "I've never worked in my life."

"Yeah," said Ronnie, "but I gotta work tonight."

"Be sure you do a good job, baby," said Curt.

"I always do a good job."

They were quiet and sat drinking their beer. Then Ronnie said, "All right, where's the god damned money?"

"You'll get it, you'll get it," said Bill. "It's lucky I brought an extra $500."

"I want it now. All of it."

"Give him the money, Bill. And while you're at it, give me mine."

It was all in hundreds. Bill counted it under the table. Ronnie got his first, then Curt got his. They checked it. O.k.

"Where's it at?" asked Ronnie.

"Here," said Bill, handing him an envelope. "The address and key are inside."

"How far away is it?"

"Thirty minutes. You take the Ventura freeway."

"Can I ask you one thing?"

"Sure."

"Why?"

"Why?"

"Yes, why?"

"Do you care?"
"No."
"Then why ask?"
"Too much beer, I guess."
"Maybe you better get going," said Curt.
"Just one more pitcher of beer," said Ronnie.
"No," said Curt, "get going."
"Well, shit, all right."

Ronnie moved around the table, got out, walked to the exit. Curt and Bill sat there looking at him. He walked outside. Night. Stars. Moon. Traffic. His car. He unlocked it, got in, drove off.

Ronnie checked the street carefully and the address more carefully. He parked a block and a half away and walked back. The key fit the door. He opened it and walked in. There was a T.V. set going in the front room. He walked across the rug.

"Bill?" somebody asked. He listened for the voice. She was in the bathroom. "Bill?" she said again. He pushed the door open and there she sat in the tub, very blond, very white, young. She screamed.

He got his hands around her throat and pushed her under the water. His sleeves were soaked. She kicked and struggled violently. It got so bad that he had to get in the tub with her, clothes and all. He had to hold her down. Finally she was still and he let her go.

Bill's clothes didn't quite fit him but at least they were dry. The wallet was wet but he kept the wallet. Then he got out of there, walked the block and one half to his car and drove off.

THIS IS WHAT KILLED DYLAN THOMAS

This is what killed Dylan Thomas.

I board the plane with my girlfriend, the sound man, the camera man and the producer. The camera is working. The sound man has attached little microphones to my girlfriend and myself. I am on my way to San Francisco to give a poetry reading. I am Henry Chinaski, poet. I am profound, I am magnificent. Balls. Well, yes, I do have magnificent balls.

Channel 15 is thinking of doing a documentary on me. I have on a clean new shirt, and my girlfriend is vibrant, magnificent, in her early thirties. She sculpts, writes, and makes marvelous love. The camera pokes into my face. I pretend it isn't there. The passengers watch, the stewardesses beam, the land is stolen from the Indians, Tom Mix is dead, and I've had a fine breakfast.

But I can't help thinking of the years in lonely rooms when the only people who knocked were the landladies asking for the back rent, or the F.B.I. I lived with rats and mice and wine and my blood crawled the walls in a world I couldn't understand and still can't. Rather than live their life, I starved; I ran inside my own mind and hid. I pulled down all the shades and stared at the ceiling. When I went out it was to a bar where I begged drinks, ran errands, was beaten in alleys by well-fed and secure men, by dull and comfortable men. Well, I won a few fights but only because I was crazy. I went for years without women, I lived on peanut butter and stale bread and boiled potatoes. I was the fool, the dolt, the idiot. I wanted to write but the typer was always in hock. I gave it up and drank. . . .

The plane rose and the camera went on. The girlfriend and I

talked. The drinks arrived. I had poetry, and a fine woman. Life was picking up. But the traps, Chinaski, watch the traps. You fought a long fight to put the word down the way you wanted. Don't let a little adulation and a movie camera pull you out of position. Remember what Jeffers said—even the strongest men can be trapped, like God when he once walked on earth.

Well, you ain't God, Chinaski, relax and have another drink. Maybe you ought to say something profound for the sound man? No, let him sweat. Let them all sweat. It's their film burning. Check the clouds for size. You're riding with executives from I.B.M., from Texaco, from . . .

You're riding with the enemy.

On the escalator out of the airport a man asks me, "What's all the cameras? What's going on?"

"I'm a poet," I tell him.

"A poet?" he asks, "what's your name?"

"Garcia Lorca," I say. . . .

Well, North Beach is different. They're young and they wear jeans and they wait around. I'm old. Where's the young ones of 20 years ago? Where's Joltin' Joe? All that. Well, I was in S.F. 30 years ago and I avoided North Beach. Now I'm walking through it. I see my face on posters all about. Be careful, old man, the suck is on. They want your blood.

My girlfriend and I walk along with Marionetti. Well, here we are walking along with Marionetti. It's nice being with Marionetti, he has very gentle eyes and the young girls stop him on the street and talk to him. Now, I think, I could stay in San Francisco . . . but I know better; it's back to L.A. for me with that machinegun mounted in the front court window. They might have caught God, but Chinaski gets advice from the devil.

Marionetti leaves and there's a beatnick coffeeshop. I have never been in a beatnick coffeeshop. I am in a beatnick coffeeshop. My girl and I get the best—60 cents a cup. Big time. It isn't worth it. The kids sit about sipping at their coffees and waiting for it to happen. It isn't going to happen.

We walk across the street to an Italian cafe. Marionetti is back with the guy from the *S. F. Chronicle* who wrote in his column that I was the best short story writer to come along since Hemingway. I tell him he is wrong; I don't know who is the best since Hemingway but it isn't H.C. I'm too careless. I don't put out enough effort. I'm tired.

The wine comes on. Bad wine. The lady brings in soup, salad, a bowl of raviolis. Another bottle of bad wine. We are too full to eat the main course. The talk is loose. We don't strain to be brilliant. Maybe we can't be. We get out.

I walk behind them up the hill. I walk with my beautiful girlfriend. I begin to vomit. Bad red wine. Salad. Soup. Raviolis. I always vomit before a reading. It's a good sign. The edge is on. The knife is in my gut while I walk up the hill.

They put us in a room, leave us a few bottles of beer. I glance over my poems. I am terrified. I heave in the sink, I heave in the toilet, I heave on the floor. I am ready.

The biggest crowd since Yevtushenko . . . I walk on stage. Hot shit. Hot shit Chinaski. There is a refrigerator full of beer behind me. I reach in and take one. I sit down and begin to read. They've paid $2 a head. Fine people, those. Some are quite hostile from the outset. 1/3 of them hate me, 1/3 of them love me, the other 3rd don't know what the hell. I have some poems that I know will increase the hate. It's good to have hostility, it keeps the head loose.

"Will Laura Day please stand up? Will my love please stand up?"

She does, waving her arms.

I begin to get more interested in the beer than the poetry. I talk between the poems, dry and banal stuff, drab. I am H. Bogart. I am Hemingway. I am hot shit.

"Read the poems, Chinaski!" they scream.

They are right, you know. I try to stay with the poems. But I'm at the refrigerator door much of the time too. It makes the work easier, and they've already paid. I'm told once John Cage came out on stage, ate an apple, walked off, got one thousand dollars. I figured I had a few beers coming.

Well, it was over. They came around. Autographs. They'd come from Oregon, L.A., Washington. Nice pretty little girls too. This is what killed Dylan Thomas.

Back upstairs at the place, drinking beer and talking to Laura and Joe Krysiak. They are beating on the door downstairs. "Chinaski! Chinaski!" Joe goes down to hold them off. I'm a rock star. Finally I go down and let some of them in. I know some of them.

Starving poets. Editors of little magazines. Some get through that I don't know. All right, all right—lock the door!

We drink. We drink. We drink. Al Masantic falls down in the bathroom and crashes the top of his head open. A very fine poet, that Al.

Well, everybody is talking. It's just another sloppy beerdrunk. Then the editor of a little magazine starts beating on a fag. I don't like it. I try to separate them. A window is broken. I push them down the steps. I push everybody down the steps, except Laura. The party is over. Well, not quite. Laura and I are into it. My love and I are into it. She's got a temper, I've got one to match. It's over nothing, as usual. I tell her to get the hell out. She does.

I wake up hours later and she's standing in the center of the room. I leap out of bed and cuss her. She's on me.

"I'll kill you, you son of a bitch!"

I'm drunk. She's on top of me on the kitchen floor. My face is bleeding. She bites a hole in my arm. I don't want to die. I don't want to die! Passion be damned! I run into the kitchen and pour half a bottle of iodine over my arm. She's throwing my shorts and shirts out of her suitcase, taking her airplane ticket. She's on her way again. We're finished forever again. I go back to bed and listen to her heels going down the hill.

On the plane back the camera is going. Those guys from Channel 15 are going to find out about life. The camera zooms in on the hole in my arm. There is a double shot in my hand.

"Gentlemen," I say, "there is no way to make it with the female. There is absolutely no way."

They all nod in agreement. The sound man nods, the camera man nods, the producer nods. Some of the passengers nod. I drink heavily all the way in, savoring my sorrow, as they say. What can a poet do without pain? He needs it as much as his typewriter.

Of course, I make the airport bar. I would have made it anyhow. The camera follows me into the bar. The guys in the bar look around, lift their drinks and talk about how impossible it is to make it with the female.

My take for the reading is $400.

"What's the camera for?" asks the guy next to me.

"I'm a poet," I tell him.

"A poet?" he asks. "What's your name?"

"Dylan Thomas," I say.

I lift my drink, empty it with one gulp, stare straight ahead. I'm on my way.

NO NECK AND BAD AS HELL

I had a jumpy stomach and she took pictures of me sweating and dying in the waiting area as I watched a plump girl in a short purple dress and high heels shoot down a row of plastic ducks with a gun. I told Vicki I'd be back and I asked the girl at the counter for a paper cup and some water and I dropped my Alka Seltzers in. I sat back down and sweated.

Vicki was happy. We were getting out of town. I liked Vicki to be happy. She deserved her happiness. I got up and went to the men's room and had a good crap. When I got out they were calling the passengers. It wasn't a very large seaplane. Two propellers. We were on last. It only held six or seven.

Vicki sat in the co-pilot's seat and they made me a seat out of the thing that folded over the door. There we went! FREEDOM. My seatbelt didn't work.

There was a Japanese guy looking at me. "My seatbelt doesn't work," I told him. He grinned back at me, happily. "Suck shit, baby," I told him. Vicki kept looking back and smiling. She was happy, a kid with candy—a 35 year old seaplane.

It took twelve minutes and we hit the water. I hadn't heaved. I got out. Vicki told me all about it. "The plane was built in 1940. It had holes in the floor. He worked the rudder with a handle from the roof. 'I'm scared,' I told him, and he said, 'I'm scared too.' "

I depended on Vicki for all my information. I wasn't much good at talking to people. Well, then we packed onto a bus, sweating and giggling and looking at each other. From the end of the bus line to the hotel was about two blocks and Vicki kept me informed: "There's a place to eat, and there's a liquor store for you, there's a bar, and there's a place to eat, and there's another liquor store . . ."

The room was all right, in front, right over the water. The T.V. worked in a vague and hesitant way and I flopped on the bed and watched while Vicki unpacked. "Oh, I just love this place!" she said, "don't you?"

"Yes."

I got up and went downstairs and across the street and got beer and ice. I packed the ice in the sink and sunk the beer in. I drank 12 bottles of beer, had a minor argument of some sort with Vicki after the tenth beer, drank the other two and went to sleep.

When I woke up, Vicki had bought an ice chest and was drawing on the cover. Vicki was a child, a Romantic, but I loved her for it. I had so many gloomy devils in me that I welcomed it.

"July 1972. Avalon Catalena" she printed on the chest. She didn't know how to spell. Well, none of us did.

Then she drew me, and underneath: "No neck and bad as hell."

Then she drew a lady, and underneath: "Henry knows a good ass when he sees one."

And in a circle: "Only God knows what he does with his nose."

And: "Chinaski has gorgeous legs."

She also drew a variety of birds and suns and stars and palm trees and the ocean.

"Are you able to eat breakfast?" she asked. I'd never been spoiled by any of my past women. I liked being spoiled; I felt that I deserved to be spoiled. We went and found a fairly reasonable place where you could eat at a table outside. Over breakfast she asked me, "Did you really win the Pulitzer Prize?"

"What Pulitzer Prize?"

"You told me last night you'd won the Pulitzer Prize. $500,000. You said you got a purple telegram about it."

"A purple telegram?"

"Yes, you said you'd beat out Norman Mailer, Kenneth Koch, Diane Wakoski, and Robert Creeley."

We finished breakfast and walked around. The whole place didn't add up to more than five or six blocks. Everybody was seventeen years old. They sat listlessly waiting. Not everybody. There were a few tourists, old, determined to have a good time. They peered angrily into shop windows and walked, stamping the pavements, giving off their rays: I have money, we have money, we have more money than you have, we are better than you are, nothing worries us; everything is shit but we are not shit and we know everything, look at us.

With their pink shirts and green shirts and blue shirts, and square white rotting bodies, and striped shorts, eyeless eyes and mouthless mouths, they walked along, very colorful, as if color might wake up death and turn it into life. They were a carnival of American decay on parade and they had no idea of the atrocity that they had inflicted upon themselves.

I left Vicki, went upstairs, crouched over the typewriter, and looked out the window. It was hopeless. All my life I had wanted to be a writer and now I had my chance and it wouldn't come. There were no bullrings and boxing matches or young señoritas. There weren't even any insights. I was fucked. I couldn't get the word down and they'd backed me into a corner. Well, all you had to do was die. But I'd always imagined it differently. I mean, the writing. Maybe it was the Leslie Howard movie. Or reading about the life of Hemingway or D. H. Lawrence. Or Jeffers. You could get started writing in all sorts of different ways. And then you wrote a while. And met some of the writers. The good ones and the bad ones. And they all had tinkertoy souls. You knew it when you got into a room with them. There was only one great writer every 500 years, and you weren't the one, and they most certainly weren't the ones. We were fucked.

I turned on the T.V. and watched a bag of doctors and nurses spew their love-troubles. They never touched. No wonder they were in trouble. All they did was talk, argue, bitch, search. I went to sleep.

Vicki woke me up. "Oh," she said, "I had the most wonderful time!"

"Yes?"

"I saw this man in a boat and I said 'Where are you going?' and he said, 'I'm a boat taxi, I take people in and out to their boats,' and I said, 'o.k.' and it was just fifty cents and I rode around with him for hours while he took people to their boats. It was wonderful."

"I watched some doctors and nurses," I said, "and I got depressed."

"We boated for hours," said Vicki, "I gave him my hat to wear and he waited while I got an abalone sandwich. He skinned his leg when he fell off his motorcycle last night."

"The bells ring here every fifteen minutes. It's obnoxious."

"I got to look in all the boats. All the old drunks were on board. Some of them had young women dressed in boots. Others had young men. Real old drunken lechers."

If I only had Vicki's ability to gather information, I thought, I could really write something. Me: I've got to sit around and wait for it to come to me. I can manipulate it and squeeze it once it arrives but I can't go find it. All I can write about is drinking beer, going to the racetrack, and listening to symphony music. That isn't a crippled life, but it's hardly all of it either. How did I get so limited? I used to have guts. What happened to my guts? Do men really get old?

"After I got off the boat I saw a bird. I talked to it. Do you mind if I buy the bird?"

"No, I don't mind. Where is it?"

"Just a block away. Can we go see him?"

"Why not?"

I got into some clothes and we walked down. Here was this shot of green with a little red ink spilled over him. He wasn't very much, even for a bird. But he didn't shit every three minutes like the rest of them, so that was pleasant.

"He doesn't have any neck. He's just like you. That's why I want him. He's a peach-faced love-bird."

We came back with the peach-faced love-bird in a cage. We put him on the table and she called him "Avalon." Vicki sat and talked to him.

"Avalon, hello Avalon . . . Avalon, Avalon, hello Avalon . . . Avalon, o, Avalon . . ."

I turned on the T.V.

The bar was all right. I sat with Vicki and told her I was going to break the place up. I used to break up bars in my early days, now I just talked about breaking them up.

There was a band. I got up and danced. It was easy to dance modern. You just kicked your arms and legs in any direction, either held your neck stiff or whipped it like a son of a bitch and they thought you were great. You could fool people. I danced and worried about my typewriter.

I sat down with Vicki and ordered some more drinks. I grabbed Vicki's head and pointed her toward the bartender. "Look, she's beautiful, man! Isn't she beautiful?"

Then Ernie Hemingway walked up with his white rat beard.

"Ernie," I said, "I thought you did it with a shotgun?"

Hemingway laughed.

"What are you drinking?" I asked.

"I'm buying," he said.

Ernie bought us our drinks and sat down. He looked a little thinner.

"I reviewed your last book," I told him. "I gave it a bad review. Sorry."

"It's all right," said Ernie. "How do you like the island?"

"It's for them," I said.

"Meaning?"

"The public is fortunate. Everything pleases them: icecream cones, rock concerts, singing, swinging, love, hate, masturbation, hot dogs, country dances, Jesus Christ, roller skating, spiritualism, capitalism, communism, circumcision, comic strips, Bob Hope, skiing, fishing murder bowling debating, anything. They don't expect much and they don't get much. They are one grand gang."

"That's quite a speech."

"That's quite a public."

"You talk like a character out of early Huxley."

"I think you're wrong. I'm desperate."

"But," said Hemingway, "men become intellectuals in order not to be desperate."

"Men become intellectuals because they are afraid, not desperate."

"And the difference between afraid and desperate is . . ."

"Bingo!" I answered, "an intellectual! . . . my drink . . ."

A little later I told Hemingway about my purple telegram and then Vicki and I left and went back to our bird and our bed.

"It's no use," I said, "my stomach is raw and contains nine tenths of my soul."

"Try this," said Vicki and handed me the glass of water and Alka Seltzer.

"You go and toddle around," I said, "I can't make it today."

Vicki went out and toddled and came back two or three times

to see if I was all right. I was all right. I went out and ate and came back with two six-packs and found an old movie with Henry Fonda, Tyrone Power, and Randolph Scott. 1939. They were all so young. It was incredible. I was seventeen years old then. But, of course, I'd come through better than them. I was still alive.

Jesse James. The acting was bad, very bad. Vicki came back and told me all sorts of amazing things and then she got on the bed with me and watched *Jesse James.* When Bob Ford was about to shoot Jesse (Ty Power) in the back, Vicki let out a moan and ran in the bathroom and hid. Ford did his thing.

"It's all over," I said, "you can come out now."

That was the highlight of the trip to Catalina. Not much else happened. Before we left Vicki went to the Chamber of Commerce and thanked them for giving her such a good time. She also thanked the woman in Davey Jones' Locker and bought presents for her friends Lita and Walter and Ava and her son Mike and something for me and something for Annie and something for a Mr. and Mrs. Croty, and there were some others I have forgotten.

We got on the boat with our bird cage and our bird and our ice chest and our suitcase and our electric typewriter. I found a spot at the back of the boat and we sat there and Vicki was sad because it was over. I had met Hemingway in the street and he had given me the hippie handshake and he asked me if I was Jewish and if I was coming back, and I said no on the Jewish and I didn't know if I was coming back, it was up to the lady, and he said, I don't want to inquire into your personal business, and I said, Hemingway you sure talk funny, and the whole boat leaned to the left and rocked and leaped and a young man who looked as if he had recently had electro-therapy treatment walked around passing out paper bags for the purpose of vomiting. I thought, maybe the seaplane's best, it's only twelve minutes and far less people, and San Pedro slowly worked toward us, civilization, civilization, smog and murder, so much nicer so much nicer, the madmen and the drunks are the last saints left on earth. I have never ridden a horse or bowled, nor have I seen the Swiss Alps, and Vicki looked over at me with this very childish smile, and I thought, she really is an amazing woman, well, it's time I had a little luck, and I stretched my legs and looked straight ahead. I needed to take another shit and decided to cut down on my drinking.

THE WAY THE DEAD LOVE

1.

It was a hotel near the top of a hill, just enough tilt in that hill to help you run down to the liquor store, and coming back with the bottle, just enough climb to make the effort worthwhile. The hotel had once been painted a peacock green, lots of hot flare, but now after the rains, the peculiar Los Angeles rains that clean and fade everything, the hot green was just hanging on by its teeth—like the people who lived inside.

How I moved in there, or why I'd left the previous place, I hardly remember. It was probably my drinking and not working very much, and the loud mid-morning arguments with the ladies of the street. And by midmorning arguments I do not mean 10:30 a.m., I mean 3:30 a.m. Usually if the police weren't called it ended up with a little note under the door, always in pencil on torn lined paper: "*dear Sir, we are going to have to ask you to move quick as poscible.*" One time it happened in mid-afternoon. The argument was over. We swept up the broken glass, put all the bottles into paper sacks, emptied the ashtrays, slept, woke up, and I was working away on top when I heard a key in the door. I was so surprised that I just kept fanning it in. And there he stood, the little manager, about 45, no hair except maybe around his ears or balls, and he looked at her on the bottom, walked up and pointed, "You—you are OUT OF HERE!" I stopped stroking and laid flat, looking at him sideways. Then he pointed at me. "And YOU'RE outa here too!" He turned around, went to the door, closed it quietly and walked down the hall. I started the machine again and we gave it a farewell good one.

Anyway, there I was, the green hotel, the faded green hotel, and

I was there with my suitcase full of rags, alone at the time, but I had the rent money, was sober, and I got a room in the front facing the street, 3rd floor, phone outside my door in the hall, hotplate in the window, large sink, small wall refrigerator, a couple of chairs, a table, bed, and the bathroom down the hall. And although the building was very old, they even had an elevator—it had once been a class joint. Now I was there. The first thing I did was get a bottle and after a drink and killing two roaches I felt like I belonged. Then I went to the phone and tried to call a lady who I felt might help me but she was evidently out helping somebody else.

2.

About 3 a.m. somebody knocked. I put on my torn bathrobe and opened the door. There stood a woman in her bathrobe. "Yeah?" I said. "Yeah?"

"I'm your neighbor. I'm Mitzi. I live down the hall. I saw you at the telephone today."

"Yeah?" I said.

Then she came around from behind her back and showed it to me. It was a pint of good whiskey.

"Come on in," I said.

I cleaned out two glasses, opened the pint. "Straight or mixed?"

"About two thirds water."

There was a litle mirror over the sink and she stood there rolling her hair into curlers. I handed her a glass of stuff and sat down on the bed.

"I saw you in the hall. I could tell by looking at you that you were nice. I can tell them. Some of them here are not so nice."

"They tell me I am a bastard."

"I don't believe it."

"Neither do I."

I finished my drink. She just sipped on hers so I mixed myself another. We talked easy talk. I had a third drink. Then I got up and stood behind her.

"OOOOOOh! Silly *boy*!"

I jabbed her.

"Ooouch!! You ARE a bastard!"

She had a curler in one hand. I pulled her up and kissed that thin little old lady's mouth. It was soft and open. She was ready. I put her drink in her hand, took her to the bed, sat her down. "Drink up." She did. I walked over and fixed her another. I didn't have anything on under my robe. The robe fell open and the thing stuck out. God, I'm filthy, I thought. I'm a ham. I'm in the movies. The family movies of the future. 2490 A.D. I had difficulty not laughing at myself, walking around hung to that stupid prong. It was really the whiskey I wanted. A castle in the hills I wanted. A steam bath. Anything but this. We both sat with our drinks. I kissed her again, ramming my cigarette-sick tongue down her throat. I came up for air. I opened her robe and there were her breasts. Not much, poor thing. I reached down with my mouth and got one. It stretched and sagged like a balloon half-filled with stale air. I braved on and sucked at the nipple as she took the prong in her hand and arched her back. We fell backwards like that on the cheap bed, and with our robes on, I took her there.

3.

His name was Lou, he was an ex-con and ex-hard rock miner. He lived downstairs in the hotel. His last job had been scrubbing out pots in a place that made candy. He had lost that one—like all the others—drinking. The unemployment insurance runs out and there we are like rats—rats with no place to hide, rats with rent to pay, with bellies that get hungry, cocks that get hard, spirits that get tired, and no education, no trade. Tough shit, like they say, this is America. We didn't want much and we couldn't get that. Tough shit.

I met Lou while drinking, people walking in and out. My room was the party room. Everybody came. There was an Indian, Dick, who shoplifted halfpints and stored them in his dresser. Said it gave him a feeling of security. When we couldn't get a drink anywhere we always used the Indian as our last resort.

I wasn't very good at shoplifting but I did learn a trick from Alabam, a thin mustached thief who had once worked for the hospital as an orderly. You throw your meats and valuables into a large sack and then cover them with potatoes. The grocer weighs the lot and charges you for potatoes. But I was best at getting Dick for credit. There were a lot of Dicks in that neighborhood and the liquor store man was a Dick too. We'd be sitting around and the last drink would be gone. My first move would be to send somebody out. "My name's Hank," I'd tell the guy. "Tell Dick, Hank sent you down for a pint on the cuff, and if there's any questions to phone me." "O.k., o.k.," and the guy would go. We'd wait, already tasting the drink, smoking pacing going crazy. Then the guy would come back. "Dick said 'no!' Dick said your credit's no good anymore!"

"SHIT!" I would scream.

And I would rise in full red-eyed unshaven indignation. "GOD DAMN, SHIT, THAT MOTHER!"

I would really be angry, it was an honest anger, I don't know where it came from. I'd slam the door, take the elevator down and down that hill I'd go . . . dirty mother, that dirty mother! . . . and I'd turn into the liquor store.

"All right, Dick."

"Hello, Hank."

"I want TWO FIFTHS!" (and I'd name a very good brand.) "Two packs of smokes, a couple of those cigars, and let's see . . . a can of those peanuts, yeah."

Dick would line the stuff up in front of me and then he'd stand there.

"Well, ya gonna pay me?"

"Dick, I want this on the bill."

"You already owe me $23.50. You used to pay me, you used to pay a little every week, I remember it was every Friday night. You ain't paid me anything in three weeks. You aren't like those other bums. You got class. I trust you. Can't you just pay me a dollar now and then?"

"Look, Dick, I don't feel like arguing. You gonna put this stuff in a bag or do you want it BACK?"

Then I'd shove the bottles and stuff toward him and wait, puffing on a cigarette like I owned the world. I didn't have any more class than a grasshopper. I felt nothing but fear that he'd do the sensible thing and put the bottles back on the shelf and tell me to go to hell. But his face would always sag and he'd put the stuff in the bag, and then I'd wait until he totalled the new bill. He'd give me the count; I'd nod and walk out. The drinks always tasted much better under those circumstances. And when I'd walk in with the stuff for the boys and girls, I was really king.

I was sitting with Lou one night in his room. He was a week behind in his rent and mine was due. We were drinking port wine. We were even rolling our cigarettes. Lou had a machine for that and they came out pretty good. The thing was to keep four walls around you. If you had four walls you had a chance. Once you were out on the street you had no chance, they had you, they really had you. Why steal something if you can't cook it? How are you going to screw something if you live in an alley? How are you going to sleep when everybody in the Union Rescue Mission snores? And steals your shoes? And stinks? And is insane? You can't even jack-off. You need four walls. Give a man four walls long enough and it is possible for him to own the world. So we were a little worried. Every step sounded like the landlady's. And she was a very mysterious landlady. A young blonde nobody could screw. I played her very cold thinking she would come to me. She came and knocked all right, but only for the rent. She had a husband somewhere but we never saw him. They lived there and they didn't. We were on the plank. We figured if we could fuck the landlady our troubles would be over. It was one of those buildings where you screwed every woman as a matter of course, almost as a matter of obligation. But I couldn't get this one and it made me feel insecure. So we sat there smoking our rolled cigarettes, drinking our port wine and the four walls were dissolving, falling away. Talk is best at times like that. You talk wild, drink your wine. We were cowards because we wanted to live. We did not want to live too badly but we still wanted to live.

"Well," said Lou, "I think I got it."

"Yeah?"

"Yeah."

I poured another wine.

"We work together."

"Sure."

"Now you're a good talker, you tell a lot of interesting stories, it doesn't matter if they're true or not—"

"They're true."

"I mean, that doesn't matter. You got a good mouth. Now here's what we do. There's a class bar down the street, you know it, Molino's. You go in there. All you need is money for the first drink. We'll pool for that. You sit down, nurse your drink and look around for a guy flashing a roll. They get some fat ones in there. You spot the guy and go over to him. You sit down next to him and turn it on, you turn on the bullshit. He'll like it. You've even got a vocabulary. O.k. so he'll buy you drinks all night, he'll drink all night. Keep him drinking. When closing time comes, you lead him toward Alvarado Street, lead him west past the alley. Tell him you are going to get him some nice young pussy, tell him anything but lead him west. And I'll be waiting in the alley with this."

Lou reached around behind the door and came out with a baseball bat, it was a very large baseball bat, I think at least 42 oz.

"Jesus Christ, Lou, you'll kill him!"

"No, no, you can't kill a drunk, you know that. Maybe if he was sober it'd kill him, but drunk it'll only knock him out. We take the wallet, split it two ways."

"Listen, Lou, I'm a nice guy, I'm not like that."

"You're no nice guy; you're the meanest son of a bitch I ever met. That's why I like you."

4.

I found one. A big fat one. I had been fired by fat stupidities like him all my life. From worthless, underpaid, dull hard jobs. It was going to be nice. I got to talking. I didn't know what I was talking about. He was listening and laughing and nodding his head and buying drinks. He had a wrist watch, a handful of rings, a full stupid wallet. It was hard work. I told him stories about prisons, about railroad track gangs, about whorehouses. He liked the whorehouse stuff.

I told him about the guy who came in every two weeks and paid well. All he wanted was a whore in a room with him. They both took off their clothes and played cards and talked. Just sat there. Then after about two hours he'd get up, get dressed, say goodbye and walk out. Never touch the whore.

"God damn," he said.

"Yeah."

I decided that I wouldn't mind Lou's slugger bat hitting a homer on that fat skull. What a whammy. What a useless hunk of shit.

"You like young girls?" I asked him.

"Oh, yeah, yeah, yeah."

"Around fourteen and a half?"

"Oh jesus, yes."

"There's one coming in on the 1:30 a.m. train from Chicago. She'll be at my place around 2:10 a.m. She's clean, hot, intelligent. Now I'm takin' a big chance, so I'm asking ten bucks. That too high?"

"No, that's all right."

"O.k., when this place closes up you come with me."

2 a.m. finally made it, and I walked him out of there, toward the alley. Maybe Lou wouldn't be there. Maybe the wine would get to him or he'd just back out. A blow like that could kill a man. Or make him addled for life. We staggered along in the moonlight. There was nobody else around, nobody in the streets. It was going to be easy.

We crossed into the alley. Lou was there. But Fatso saw him. He threw up an arm and ducked as Lou swung. The bat got me right behind the ear.

5.

Lou got his old job back, the one he had lost drinking, and he swore he was only going to drink on weekends.

"O.k., friend," I told him, "stay away from me, I am drunk and drinking all the time."

"I know, Hank, and I like you, I like you better than any man I ever met, only I gotta hold the drinking down to weekends, just Friday and Saturday nights and nothing on Sunday. I kept missing Monday mornings in the old days and it cost me my job. I'll stay away but I want you to know that it has nothing to do with you."

"Only that I'm a wino."

"Yeah, well, there's that."

"O.k., Lou, just don't come knocking on my door until Friday and Saturday night. You may hear singing and the laughter of beautiful seventeen year old girls but don't come knocking on my door."

"Man, you screw nothing but bags."

"They look seventeen through the eye of the grape."

He went on to explain the nature of his job, something to do with cleaning out the inside of candy machines. It was a sticky dirty job. The boss only hired ex-cons and worked their asses to death. He cussed the ex-cons brutally all day long and there was nothing they could do about it. He shorted them on their checks and there was nothing they could do about it. If they bitched they were fired. A lot of them were on parole. The boss had them by the balls.

"Sounds like a guy who needs to be killed," I told Lou.

"Well, he likes me, he says I am the best worker he ever had, but I hadda get off the booze, he needed somebody he could depend on. He even had me over to his place one time to do some painting for him, I painted his bathroom, did a good job too. He's got a place in the hills, a big place, and you oughta see his wife. I never knew they made women that way, so beautiful—her eyes, her legs, her body, the way she walked, talked, jesus."

6.

Well, Lou was true to his word. I didn't see him for some time, not even on weekends, and meanwhile I was going through a kind of personal hell. I was very jumpy, nerves gone—a little noise and I'd jump out of my skin. I was afraid to go to sleep: nightmare after nightmare, each more terrible than the one which preceded it. You were all right if you went to sleep totally drunk, that was all right, but if you went to sleep half-drunk or, worse, sober, then the dreams began, only you were never sure whether you were sleeping or whether the action was taking place in the room, for when you slept you dreamed the entire room, the dirty dishes, the mice, the folding walls, the pair of shit-in pants some whore had left on the floor, the dripping faucet, the moon like a bullet out there, cars full of the sober and well-fed, shining headlights through your window, everything, everything, you were in some sort of dark corner, dark dark, no help, no reason, no no reason at all, dark sweating corner, darkness and filth, the stench of reality, the stink of everything: spiders, eyes, landladies, sidewalks, bars, buildings, grass, no grass, light, no light, nothing belonging to you. The pink elephants never showed up but plenty of little men with savage tricks or a looming big man to strangle you or sink his teeth into the back of your neck, lay on your back and you sweating, unable to move, this black stinking hairy thing laying there on you on you on you.

If it wasn't that it was sitting during the days, hours of unspeakable fear, fear opening in the center of you like a giant blossom, you couldn't analyze it, figure why it was there, and that made it worse. Hours of sitting in a chair in the middle of a room, run through and stricken. Shitting or pissing a major effort, nonsense, and combing your hair or brushing your teeth—ridiculous and insane acts. Walking through a sea of fire. Or pouring water into a drinking glass—it seemed you had no right to pour water into a drinking glass. I decided I was crazy, unfit, and this made me feel dirty. I went to the library and tried to find books about what made people feel the way I was feeling, but the books weren't there or if they were I couldn't understand them. Going into the library was hardly easy—everybody seemed so comfortable, the librarians, the readers, everybody but me. I even had trouble using the library crapper—the bums in there, the queers watching me piss, they all seemed stronger than I—unworried and sure. I kept going out and walking across the street, up a winding stairway in a cement building where they stored thousands of crates of oranges. A sign on the roof of another building said JESUS SAVES but neither Jesus or oranges were worth a damn to me walking up that winding stairway and into that cement building. I always thought, this is where I belong, inside of this cement tomb.

The thought of suicide was always there, strong, like ants running along the underside of the wrists. Suicide was the only positive thing. Everything else was negative. And there was Lou, glad to clean out the inside of candy machines to stay alive. He was wiser than I.

7.

At this time I met a lady in a bar, a little older than me, very sensible. Her legs were still good, she had an odd sense of humor, and had very expensive clothes. She had come down the ladder from some rich man. We went to my place and lived together. She was a very good piece of ass but had to drink all the time. Her name was Vicki. We screwed and drank wine, drank wine and screwed. I had a library card and went to the library every day. I hadn't told her about the suicide thing. It was always a big joke, my coming home from the library. I would open the door and she would look at me.

"What no *books*?"

"Vicki, they don't have any books in the library."

I'd come in and take the wine bottle (or bottles) out of the bag and we'd begin.

One time after a week's drinking I decided to kill myself. I didn't tell her. I figured I'd do it when she was in a bar looking for a "live one." I didn't like those fat clowns screwing her but she brought me money and whiskey and cigars. She gave me the bit about me being the only one she loved. She called me "Mr. Van Bilderass" for some reason I couldn't figure. She'd get drunk and keep saying, "You think you're hot stuff, you think you're Mr. Van Bilderass!" All the time I was working on the idea of how to kill myself. One day I was sure I would do it. It was after a week's drinking, port wine, we had bought huge jugs and lined them up on the floor and behind the huge jugs we had lined up ordinary-sized winebottles, 8 or 9 of them, and behind the ordinary-size bottles we had lined up 4 or 5 little bottles. Night and day got lost. It was just screwing and talking and drinking, talking and drinking and screwing. Violent arguments that ended in love-making. She was a sweet little pig of a screw, tight and squirming. One woman in 200. With most of the rest it is kind of an act, a joke. Anyhow, maybe because of it all, the drinking and the fact of the fat dull bulls screwing Vicki, I got very sick and depressed, and yet what the hell could I do? run a turret-lathe?

When the wine ran out the depression, the fear, the uselessness of going on became too much and I knew I was going to do it. The first time she left the room it was over for me. How, I was not quite sure but there were hundreds of ways. We had a little gas jet stove. Gas is charming. Gas is a kind of a kiss. It leaves the body whole. The wine was gone. I could hardly walk. Armies of fear and sweat ran up and down my body. It becomes quite simple. The greatest relief is never to have to pass another human being on the sidewalk, see them walking in their fat, see their little rat eyes, their cruel 2-bit faces, their animal flowering. What a sweet dream: to never have to look into another human face.

"I'm going out to look at a newspaper, to see what day it is, o.k.?"

"Sure," she said, "sure."

I walked out the door. Nobody in the hall. No humans. It was about 10 p.m. I went down in the urine-smelling elevator. It took a lot of strength to be swallowed by that elevator. I walked down the hill. When I got back she would be gone. She moved quickly when the drinks ran out. Then I could do it. But first I wanted to know what day it was. I walked down the hill and there by the drugstore was the newspaper rack. I looked at the date on the newspaper. It was a Friday. Very well, Friday. As good a day as any. That meant something. Then I read the headline:

MILTON BERLE'S COUSIN HIT ON HEAD BY
FALLING ROCK

I didn't quite get it. I leaned closer and read it again. It was the same:

MILTON BERLE'S COUSIN HIT ON HEAD BY
FALLING ROCK

This was in black type, large type, the banner headline. Of all the important things that had happened in the world, this was their headline.

MILTON BERLE'S COUSIN HIT ON HEAD BY
FALLING ROCK

I crossed the street, feeling much better, and walked into the liquor store. I got two bottles of port and a pack of cigarettes on credit. When I got back to the place Vicki was still there.

"What day is it?" she asked.

"Friday."

"O.k.," she said.

I poured two glasses full of wine. There was a little ice left in the small wall refrigerator. The cubes of ice floated smoothly.

"I don't want to make you unhappy," Vicki said.

"I know you don't."

"Have a sip first."

"Sure."

"A note came under the door while you were gone."

"Yeah."

I took a sip, gagged, lit a cigarette, took another sip, then she handed me the note. It was a warm Los Angeles night. A Friday. I read the note:

Dear Mr. Chinaski: You have until next Wednesday to get up the rent. If you don't, you are out. I know about those women in your room. And you make too much noise. And you broke your window. You are paying for your privileges. Or supposed to be. I have been very kind with you. I now say next Wednesday or you are out. The tenants are tired of all the noise and cussing and singing night and day, day and night, and so am I. You can't live here without rent. Don't say I didn't warn you.

I drank the rest of the wine down, almost lost it. It was a warm night in Los Angeles.

"I'm tired of fucking those fools," she said.

"I'll get the money," I told her.

"How? You don't know how to do anything."

"I know that."

"Then how are we going to make it?"

"Somehow."

"That last guy fucked me three times. My pussy was raw."

"Don't worry, baby, I'm a genius. The only trouble is, nobody knows it."

"A genius at *what*?"

"I don't know."

"Mr. Van Bilderass!"

"That's me. By the way, do you know that Milton Berle's cousin was hit on the head by a falling rock?"

"When?"

"Today or yesterday."

"What kind of rock?"

"I don't know. I imagine some kind of big buttery yellow stone."

"Who gives a damn?"

"Not I. Certainly not I. Except—"

"Except what?"

"Except I guess that rock kept me alive."

"You talk like an asshole."

"I am an asshole."

I grinned and poured wine all around.

ALL THE ASSHOLES IN THE WORLD AND MINE

"no man's suffering is ever larger than nature intended."
—conversation overheard at a crapgame

1.

It was the ninth race and the horse's name was Green Cheese. He won by 6 and I got back 52 for 5 and since I was far ahead anyhow, it called for another drink. "Gimme a shota green cheese," I told the barkeep. It didn't confuse him. He knew what I was drinking. I had been leaning there all afternoon. I had been drunk all the night before and when I got home, of course, I had to have some more. I was set. I had scotch, vodka, wine and beer. A mortician or somebody called about 8 p.m. and said he'd like to see me. "Fine," I said, "bring drinks." "Do you mind if I bring friends?" "I don't have any friends." "I mean my friends." "I do not give a damn," I told him. I went into the kitchen and poured a water glass ¾'s full of scotch. I drank it down straight just like the old days. I used to drink a fifth in an hour and a half, two hours. "Green cheese," I said to the kitchen walls. I opened a tall can of frozen beer.

2.

The mortician arrived and got on the phone and pretty soon many strange people were walking in, all of them bringing drinks with them. There were a lot of women and I felt like raping all of them. I sat on the rug, feeling the electric light, feeling the drinks going through me like a parade, like an attack on the blues, like an attack on madness.

"I will never have to work again!" I told them. "The horses will take care of me like no whore EVER did!"

"Oh, we *know* that Mr. Chinaski! We know that you are a GREAT man!"

It was a little greyhaired fucker on the couch, rubbing his hands, leering at me with wet lips. He meant it. He made me sick. I finished the drink in my hand and found another somewhere and drank that too. I began talking to the women. I promised them all the endearments of my mighty cock. They laughed. I meant it. Right then. There. I moved toward the women. The men pulled me off. For a worldly man I was very much the highschool boy. If I hadn't been the great Mr. Chinaski, somebody would have killed me. As it was, I ripped off my shirt and offered to go out on the lawn with anybody. I was lucky. Nobody felt like pushing me over my shoelaces.

When my mind cleared it was 4 a.m. All the lights were on and everybody was gone. I was still sitting there. I found a warm beer and drank it. Then I went to bed with the feeling that all drunks know: that I had been a fool but to hell with it.

3.

I had been bothered with hemorrhoids for 15 or 20 years; also perforated ulcers, bad liver, boils, anxiety-neurosis, various types of insanity, but you go on with things and just hope that everything doesn't fall apart at once.

It seemed that drunk almost did it. I felt dizzy and weak, but that was ordinary. It was the hemorrhoids. They would not respond to anything—hot baths, salves, nothing helped. My intestines hung almost out of my ass like a dog's tail. I went to a doctor. He simply glanced. "Operation," he said. "All right," I said, "only thing is that I am a coward."

"Vel, ya, dot vill make it more difficult."

You lousy Nazi bastard, I thought.

"I vant you to take dis laxative der Tuesday night, den at 7 a.m. you get up, ya? and you gif yourself de enema, you keep giffing dis enema until der wasser is clear, ya? den I take unudder look into you at 10 a.m. Vensday morning."

"Ya whol, mine herring," I said.

4.

The enema tube kept slipping out and the whole bathroom got wet and it was cold and my belly hurt and I was drowning in slime and shit. This is the way the world ended, not with an atom bomb, but with shit shit shit. With the set I had bought there was nothing to pinch the flow of water and my fingers would not work so the water ran in full blast and out full blast. It took me an hour and a half and by then my hemorrhoids were in command of the world. Several times I thought of just quitting and dying. I found a can of pure spirits of gum turpentine in my closet. It was a beautiful red and green can. "DANGER!" it said, "harmful or fatal if swallowed." I *was* a coward: I put the can back.

5.

The doctor put me up on a table. "Now, chust relox der bock, ya? relox, relox . . ."

Suddenly he jammed a wedge-shaped box into my ass and began unwinding his snake which began to crawl up into my intestine looking for blockage, looking for cancer.

"Ha! Now if it hurts a bit, nien? den pant like a dog, go, hahahahahaaaa!"

"You dirty motherfucker!"

"Vot?"

"Shit, shit, shit! You dog-burner! You swine, sadist . . . You burned Joan at the stake, you put nails in the hands of Christ, you voted for war, you voted for Goldwater, you voted for Nixon . . . Mother-ass! What are you DOING to me?"

"It vill soon be over. You take it vell. You will be good patient."

He rolled the snake back in and then I saw him peering into something that looked like a periscope. He slammed some gauze up my bloody ass and I got up and put on my clothes. "And the operation will be for what?"

He knew what I meant. "Chust der hemorrhoids."

I peeked up his nurse's legs as I walked out. She smiled sweetly.

6.

In the waiting room of the hospital a little girl looked at our grey faces, our white faces, our yellow faces . . . "Everybody is dying!" she proclaimed. Nobody answered her. I turned the page of an old *Time* magazine.

After routine filling out of papers . . . urine specimens . . . blood, I was taken to a four bed ward on the eighth floor. When the question of religion came up I said "Catholic," largely to save myself from the stares and questions that usually followed a proclamation of no religion. I was tired of all the arguments and red tape. It was a Catholic hospital—maybe I'd get better service or blessings from the Pope.

Well, I was locked in with three others. Me, the monk, the loner, gambler, playboy, idiot. It was all over. The beloved solitude, the refrigerator full of beer, the cigars on the dresser, the phone numbers of the big-legged, big-assed women.

There was one with a yellow face. He looked somehow like a big fat bird dipped in urine and sun-dried. He kept hitting his button. He had a whining, crying, mewing voice. "Nurse, nurse, where's Dr. Thomas? Dr. Thomas gave me some codeine yesterday. Where's Dr. Thomas?"

"I don't know where Dr. Thomas is."

"Can I have a coughdrop?"

"They are right on your table."

"They ain't stoppin' my cough, and that cough medicine ain't any good either."

"Nurse!" a whitehaired guy yelled from the northeast bed, "can I have some more coffee? I'd like some more coffee."

"I'll see," she said and left.

My window showed hills, a slope of hills rising. I looked at the slopes of hills. It was getting dark. Nothing but houses on the hills. Old houses. I had the strange feeling that they were unoccupied that everybody had died, that everybody had given up. I listened to the three men complain about the food, about the price of the ward, about the doctors and nurses. When one spoke the other two did not seem to be listening, they did not answer. Then another would begin. They took turns. There was nothing else to do. They spoke vaguely, switching subjects. I was in with an Oakie, a movie cameraman, and the yellow piss-bird. Outside of my window a cross turned in the sky—first it was blue, then it was red. It was night and they pulled our curtains around our beds a bit and I felt better, but realized, oddly, that pain or possible death did not bring me closer to humanity. Visitors began arriving. I didn't have any visitors. I felt like a saint. I looked out of my window and saw a sign near the turning red and blue cross in the sky. MOTEL, it said. Bodies in there in more gentle attunement. Fucking.

7.

A poor devil dressed in green came in and shaved my ass. Such terrible jobs in the world! There was one job I had missed.

They slipped a showercap over my head and pushed me onto a roller. This was it. Surgery. The coward gliding down the halls past the dying. There was a man and a woman. They pushed me and smiled, they seemed very relaxed. They rolled me onto an elevator. There were four women on the elevator.

"I'm going to surgery. Any of you ladies care to change places with me?"

They drew up against the wall and refused to answer.

In the operating room we awaited for the arrival of God. God finally entered: "Vell, vell, vell, dere isss mine friend!"

I didn't even bother to answer such a lie.

"Turn on der stomach, please."

"Well," I said, "I guess it's too late to change my mind now."

"Ya," said God, "you are now in our power!"

I felt the strap go across my back. They spread my legs. The first spinal went in. It felt like he was spreading towels all around my asshole and across my back. Another spinal. A third. I kept giving them lip. The coward, the showman, whistling in the dark.

"Put him to sleep, ya," he said. I felt a shot in the elbow, a stinger. No good. Too many drunks behind me.

"Anybody got a cigar?" I asked.

Somebody laughed. I was getting corny. Bad form. I decided to be quiet.

I could feel the knife tugging at my ass. There wasn't any pain.

"Now dis," I heard him say, "dis iss the main obstruction, see? und here . . ."

8.

The recovery room was dull. There were some fine-looking women walking around but they ignored me. I got up on my elbow and looked around. Bodies everywhere. Very very white and still. Real operations. Lungers. Heart cases. Everything. I felt somewhat the amateur and somewhat ashamed. I was glad when they wheeled me out of there. My three roomies really stared when they rolled me in. Bad form. I rolled off the thing onto the bed. I found that my legs were still numb and that I had no control over them. I decided to go to sleep. The whole place was depressing. When I woke up my ass was really hurting. But legs still dull. I reached down for my cock and it felt as if it wasn't there. I mean, there wasn't any feeling. Except I wanted to piss and I couldn't piss. It was horrible and I tried to forget it.

One of my ex-loves came by and sat there looking at me. I had told her I was going in. Quite what for, I don't know.

"Hi! How you doin'?"

"Fine, only I can't piss."

She smiled.

We talked a little about something and then she left.

9.

It was like in the movies: all the male nurses seemed to be homosexual. One seemed more manly than the others.

"Hey, buddy!"

He came over. "I can't piss. I want to piss but I can't."

"I'll be right back. I'll fix you up."

I waited quite a while. Then he came back, pulled the curtain around my bed and sat down.

Jesus, I thought, what's he gonna do? Gimme a head-job?

But I looked and he seemed to have some kind of machine with him. I watched as he took a hollow needle and ran it down the piss-hole of my cock. The feeling that I thought was gone from my cock was suddenly back.

"Shit o baby!" I hissed.

"Not the most pleasant thing in the world, is it?"

"Indeed, indeed. I tend to agree. *Weeowee!* Shit and jesus!"

"Soon be over."

He pressed against my bladder. I could see the little square fish-bowl filling with piss. This was one of the parts they left out of the movies.

"God o mighty, pal, mercy! Let's call it a good night's work."

"Just a moment. Now."

He drew the needle out. Out the window my blue and red cross turned, turned. Christ hung on the wall with a piece of dried palm stuck at his feet. No wonder men turned to gods. It was pretty hard to take it straight.

"Thanks," I told the nurse.

"Any time, any time." He pulled the curtain back and left with his machine.

My yellow piss-bird punched his button.

"Where's that nurse? O why o why doesn't that nurse come?"

He pushed it again.

"Is my button working? Is something wrong with my button?"

The nurse came in.

"My back hurts! O, my back hurts *terrible*! Nobody has come to visit me! I guess you fellows noticed that! Nobody has come to see me! Not even my wife! Where's my wife? Nurse, raise my bed, my back *hurts*! THERE! Higher! No, no, my god, you've got it too high! Lower, lower! There. Stop! Where's my dinner? I haven't had dinner! Look . . ."

The nurse walked out.

I keep wondering about the little pissmachine. I'll probably have to buy one, carry it around all my life. Duck into alleys, behind trees, in the back seat of my car.

The Oakie in bed one hadn't said much. "It's my foot," he suddenly said to the walls, "I can't understand it, my foot just got all swelled-up overnight and it won't go down. It hurts, it hurts."

The whitehaired guy in the corner pushed his button.

"Nurse," he said, "nurse, how about hustling me up a pot of coffee?"

Really, I though, my main problem is to keep from going insane.

10.

The next day old whitehair (the movie cameraman) brought his coffee down and sat in a chair by my bed. "I can't stand that son of a bitch." He was speaking of the yellow piss-bird. Well, there was nothing to do with whitehair but talk to him. I told him that drink had brought me pretty much to my present station in life. For kicks I told him some of my wilder drunks and some of the crazy things that had happened. He had some good ones himself.

"In the old days," he told me, "they used to have the big red cars that ran between Glendale and Long Beach, I believe it was. They ran all day and most of the night except for an interval of an hour and a half, I think between 3:30 and 5:30 a.m.. Well, I went drinking one night and met a buddy at the bar and after the bar closed we went to his place and finished something he had left there. I left his place and kinda got lost. I turned up a deadend street but I didn't know it was deadend. I kept driving and I was driving pretty fast. I kept going until I hit the railroad tracks. When I hit the tracks my steering wheel came up and hit me on the chin and knocked me out. There I was across those tracks in my car K.O.'d. Only I was lucky because it was in the hour and a half that no trains were running. I don't know how long I sat there. But the train horn woke me up. I woke up and saw this train coming down the tracks at me. I just had time to start the car and back off. The train tore on by. I drove the car home, the front wheels all bent under and wobbling."

"That's tight."

"Another time I am sitting in the bar. Right across the way is a place where the railroadmen ate. The train stopped and the men got out to eat. I am sitting next to some guy in this bar. He turns to me and he says, 'I used to drive one of those things and I can drive one again. Come on and watch me start it.' I walked out with him and we climbed into the engine. Sure enough, he started the thing. We got up good speed. Then I started thinking, what the hell am I doing? I told the guy, 'I don't know about you but I'm getting *off!*' I knew enough about trains to know where the brake was. I yanked the brake and before the train even stopped I went out the side. He went out the other side and I never saw him again. Pretty soon there is a big crowd around the train, policemen, train investigators, yard dicks, reporters, onlookers. I am standing off to one side with the rest of the crowd, watching. 'Come on, let's go up and find out what's going on!" somebody next to me said. 'Nah, hell,' I said, 'it's just a train.' I was scared that maybe somebody had seen me. The next day there was a story in the papers. The headline said, TRAIN GOES TO PACOIMA BY ITSELF. I cut out the story and saved it. I saved that clipping for ten years. My wife used to see it. 'What the hell you saving this story for?—TRAIN GOES TO PACOIMA BY ITSELF.' I never told her. I was still scared. You're the first one I ever told the story to."

"Don't worry," I told him, "not a single soul will ever hear that story again."

Then my ass really began to kick up and whitehair suggested I ask for a shot. I did. The nurse gave me one in the hip. She left the curtain pulled when she left but whitehair continued to sit there. In fact, he had a visitor. A visitor with a voice that carried clear down through my fucked-up bowels. He really sent it out.

"I'm going to move all the ships around the neck of the bay. We'll shoot it right there. We're paying a captain of one of those boats $890 a month and he has two boys under him. We've got this fleet right there. Let's put it to use, I think. The public's ready for a good sea story. They haven't had a good sea story since Errol Flynn."

"Yeah," said whitehair, "those things run in cycles. The public's ready now. They need a good sea story."

"Sure, there are lots of kids who have never seen a sea story. And speaking of kids, that's all I'm gonna use. I'll run 'em all over the boats. The only old people we'll use will be for the leads. We just move these ships around the bay and shoot right there. Two of the ships need masts, that's all that's wrong with them. We hand them masts and then we begin."

"The public is sure ready for a sea story. It's a cycle and the cycle is due."

"They are worried about the budget. Hell, it won't cost a thing. Why—"

I pulled the curtain back and spoke to whitehair. "Look, you might think me a bastard, but you guys are right against my bed. Can't you take your friend over to your bed?"

"Sure, sure!"

The producer stood up. "Hell, I'm sorry. I didn't know . . ."

He was fat and sordid; content, happy, sickening.

"O.k.," I said.

They moved up to whitehair's bed and continued to talk about the sea story. All the dying on the eighth floor of the Queen of Angels Hospital could hear the sea story. The producer finally left.

Whitehair looked over at me. "That's the world's greatest producer. He's produced more great pictures than any man alive. That was John F."

"John F.," said the piss-bird, "yeah, he's made some great pictures, great pictures!"

I tried to go to sleep. It was hard to sleep at night because they all snored. At once. Whitehair was the loudest. In the morning he always woke me up to complain that he hadn't slept. That night the yellow piss-bird hollered all night. First because he couldn't shit. Unplug me, my god, I gotta crap! Or he hurt. Or where was his doctor? He kept having different doctors. One couldn't stand him and another would take over. They couldn't find anything wrong with him. There wasn't: he wanted his mother but his mother was dead.

11.

I finally got them to move me to a semi-private ward. But it was a worse move. His name was Herb and like the male nurse told me, "He's not sick. There isn't anything wrong with him at all." He had on a silk robe, shaved twice a day, had a T.V. set which he never turned off, and visitors all the time. He was head of a fairly large business and had gone the formula of having his grey hair short-cropped to indicate youth, efficiency, intelligence, and brutality.

The T.V. turned out to be far worse than I could have imagined. I had never owned a T.V. and so was unaccustomed to its fare. The auto races were all right, I could stand the auto races, although they were very dull. But there was some type of Marathon on for some Cause or another and they were collecting money. They started early in the morning and went right on through. Little numbers were posted indicating how much money had been collected. There was somebody in a cook's hat. I don't know what the hell he meant. And there was a terrible old woman with a face like a frog. She was terribly ugly. I couldn't believe it. I couldn't believe these people didn't know how ugly and naked and meaty and disgusting their faces looked—like rapes of everything decent. And yet they just walked up and calmly put their faces on the screen and spoke to each other and laughed about something. The jokes were very hard to laugh at but they didn't seem to have any trouble. Those faces, those faces! Herb didn't say anything about it. He just kept looking as if he were interested. I didn't know the names of the people but they were all stars of some sort. They'd announce a name and then everybody would get excited—except me. I couldn't understand it. I got a little sick. I wished I were back in the other room. Meanwhile, I was trying to have my first bowel movement. Nothing happened. A swath of blood. It was Saturday night. The priest came by. "Would you care for Communion tomorrow?" he asked. "No, thank you, Father, I'm not a very good Catholic. I haven't been to church in 20 years." "Were you baptized a Catholic?" "Yes." "Then you're still a Catholic. You're just a bum Catholic." Just like in the movies—he talks turkey, just like Cagney, or was it Pat O'Brien who sported the white collar? All my movies were dated: the last movie I had seen was *The Lost Weekend.* He gave me a little booklet. "Read this." He left.

PRAYER BOOK, it said. *Compiled for use in hospitals and institutions.*

I read.

O Eternal and ever-blessed Trinity, Father, Son, and Holy Ghost, with all the angels and saints, I adore you.

My Queen and my Mother, I give myself entirely to you; and to show my devotion to you, I consecrate to you this day my eyes, my ears, my mouth, my heart, my whole being without reserve.

Agonizing Heart of Jesus, have mercy on the dying.

O my God, prostrate on my knees, I adore you . . .

Join me, you blessed Spirits, in thanking the God of Mercies, who is so bountiful to so unworthy a creature.

It was my sins, dear Jesus, that caused your bitter anguish . . . my sins that scourged you, and crowned you with thorns, and nailed you to the cross. I confess that I deserve only punishment.

I got up and tried to shit. It had been three days. Nothing. Only a swath of blood again and the cuts in my rectum ripping open. Herb had on a comedy show.

"The Batman is coming onto the program tonight. I wanna see the Batman!"

"Yeah?" I crawled back into bed.

I am especially sorry for my sins of impatience and anger, my sins of discouragement and rebellion.

The Batman showed up. Everybody on the program seemed excited. "It's the Batman!" said Herb.

"Good," I said, "the Batman." *Sweet Heart of Mary, be my savior.*

"He can sing! Look, he can sing!"

The Batman had removed his Batsuit and was dressed in a street-suit. He was a very ordinary looking young man with a somewhat blank face. He sang. The song lasted and lasted and the Batman seemed very proud of his singing, for some reason.

"He can sing!" said Herb.

My good God, what am I and who are you, that I should dare approach you?

I am only a poor, wretched, sinful creature, totally unworthy to appear before you.

I turned my back on the T.V. set and tried to sleep. Herb had it on very loud. I had some cotton which I stuck into my ears but it helped very little. I'll never shit, I thought, I'll never shit again, not with that thing on. It's got my guts tightened, tightened . . . I'm gonna go nuts for sure this time!

O Lord, my God, from this day I accept from your hand willingly and with submission, the kind of death that it may please you to send me, with all its sorrows, pains, and anguish. (Plenary indulgence once daily, under the usual conditions.)

Finally, at 1:30 a.m. I could submit no longer. I had been listening since 7 a.m. My shit was blocked for Eternity. I felt that I had paid for the Cross in those eighteen and one-half hours. I managed to turn around.

"Herb! For Christ's sake, man! I'm about to have it! I'm about to go off my screw! Herb! MERCY! I CAN'T STAND T.V.! I CAN'T STAND THE HUMAN RACE! Herb! Herb!"

He was asleep, sitting up.

"You dirty cunt-lapper," I said.

"Whatza? whatz??"

"WHY DON'T YOU TURN THAT THING OFF?"

"Turn . . . off? ah, sure, sure . . . whyn't ya say so, kid?"

12.

Herb snored too. He also talked in his sleep. I went to sleep about 3:30 a.m. At 4:15 a.m. I was awakened by something that sounded like a table being dragged down the hall. Suddenly the lights went on and a big colored woman was standing over me with a clipboard. Christ, she was an ugly and stupid looking wench, Martin Luther King and racial equality be damned! She could have easily beat the shit out of me. Maybe that would be a good idea? Maybe it was Last Rites? Maybe I was finished?

"Look baby," I said, "ya mind telling me what's going on? Is this the fucking end?"

"Are you Henry Chinaski?"

"I'm afraid so."

"You're down for Communion."

"No, wait! He got his signals crossed. I told him, *No Communion.*"

"Oh," she said. She pulled the curtains back and turned off the lights. I could hear the table or whatever it was going further down the hall. The Pope was going to be very unhappy with me. The table made a hell of a racket. I could hear the sick and the dying waking up, coughing, asking questions to the air, ringing for the nurses.

"What was that, kid?" Herb asked.

"What was what?"

"All that noise and lights?"

"That was the Dark Tough Angel of the Batman making ready The Body of Christ."

"What?"

"Go to sleep."

13.

My doctor came the next morning and peered up my ass and told me I could go home. "But, my boy, you do not go horseback riding, ya?"

"Ya. But how about some hot pussy?"

"Vot?"

"Sexual intercourse."

"Oh, *nein, nein*! It vill be six to eight weeks before you vill be able to resume *anything* normal."

He moved on out and I began to dress. The T.V. didn't bother me. Somebody on the screen said, "I wonder if my spaghetti is done?" He stuck his face into the pot and when he looked up, all the spaghetti was stuck to his face. Herb laughed. I shook hands with him. "So long baby," I said. "It's been nice," he said. "Yeah," I said. I was ready to leave when it happened. I ran to the can. Blood and shit. Shit and blood. It was painful enough to make me talk to the walls. "Ooo, mama, you dirty fuck bastards, oh shit shit, o you come-crazy freaks, o you shit-mauling cocksucker heavens, lay off! Shit, shit shit, YOW!"

Finally it stopped. I cleaned myself, put on a gauze bandage, pulled up my pants and walked over to my bed, picked up my traveling bag.

"So long, Herb, baby."

"So long, kid."

You guessed it. I ran in there again.

"You dirty mother-humpin' cat-fuckers! Oooooo, shitshitshit-SHIT!"

I came out and sat awhile. There was a smaller movement and then I felt that I was ready. I went downstairs and signed a fortune in bills. I couldn't read anything. They called me a taxi and I stood outside the ambulance entrance waiting. I had my little sitz bath with me. A dishpan you shit in after you filled it with hot water. There were three Oakies standing outside, two men and a woman. Their voices were loud and Southern and they had the look and feel that nothing had ever happened to them—not even a toothache. My ass began to leap and twinge. I tried to sit down but that was a mistake. They had a little boy with them. He ran up and tried to grab my dishpan. He tugged. "No, you bastard, no," I hissed at him. He almost got it. He was stronger than I was but I kept holding on.

O Jesus, I commend to you my parents, relatives, benefactors, teachers, and friends. Reward them in a very special way for all the care and sorrow I have caused them.

"You little jerkoff! Unhand my shitpot!" I told him.

"Donny! You leave that man alone!" the woman hollered at him.

Donny ran off. One of the men looked at me. "Hi!" he said. "Hi," I answered.

That cab looked good. "Chinaski?"

"Yeah. Let's go." I got in front with my shitpot. I kind of sat on one cheek. I gave him directions. Then, "Listen, if I holler pull behind a signboard, a gas station, anywhere. But stop driving. I might have to shit."

"O.k."

We drove along. The streets looked good. It was noontime. I was still alive. "Listen," I asked him, "where's a good whorehouse? Where can I pick up a good clean cheap piece of ass?"

"I don't know anything about that stuff."

"COME ON! COME ON!" I hollered at him. "Do I look like the fuzz? Do I look like a fink? You can level with me, Ace!"

"No, I'm not kidding. I don't know about that stuff. I drive daylight. Maybe a night cabbie might line you up."

"O.k., I believe you. Turn here."

The old shack looked good sitting down there between all the highrise apartments. My '57 Plymouth was covered with birdshit and the tires were half-flat. All I wanted was a hot bath. A hot bath. Hot water against my poor asshole. Quiet. The old Racing Forms. The gas and light bills. The letters from lonely women too far away to fuck. Water. Hot water. Quiet. And myself spreading through the walls, returning to the manhole of my goddamned soul. I gave him a good tip and walked slowly up the driveway. The door was open. Wide. Somebody was hammering on something. The sheets were off the bed. My god, I had been raided! I had been evicted!

I walked in. "HEY!" I hollered.

The landlord walked into the front room. "Geez, we didn't expect you back so soon! The hot water tank was leaking and we had to rip it out. We're gonna put in a new one."

"You mean, no hot water?"

"No, no hot water."

O good Jesus, I accept willingly this trial which it has pleased you to lay upon me.

His wife walked in.

"Oh, I was just gonna make your bed."

"All right. Fine."

"He should get the watertank hooked up today. We might be short of parts. It's hard to get parts on Sunday."

"O.k., I'll make the bed," I said.

"I'll get it for you."

"No, please, I'll get it."

I went into the bedroom and began making the bed. Then it came. I ran to the can. I could hear him hammering on the watertank as I sat down. I was glad he was hammering. I gave a quiet speech. Then I went to bed. I heard the couple in the next court. He was drunk. They were arguing. "The trouble with you is that you have no conceptions at all! You don't know nothing! You're stupid! And on top of that, you're a whore!"

I was home again. It was great. I rolled over on my belly. In Vietnam the armies were at it. In the alleys the bums sucked on wine bottles. The sun was still up. The sun came through the curtains. I saw a spider crawling along the windowledge. I saw an old newspaper on the floor. There was a photo of three young girls jumping a fence showing plenty of leg. The whole place looked like me and smelled like me. The wallpaper knew me. It was perfect. I was conscious of my feet and my elbows and my hair. I did not feel 45 years old. I felt like a goddamned monk who had just had a revelation. I felt as if I were in love with something that was very good but I was not sure what it was except that it was there. I listened to all the sounds, the sounds of motorcycles and cars. I heard dogs barking. People and laughing. Then I slept. I slept and I slept and I slept. While a plant looked through my window, while a plant looked at me. The sun went on working and the spider crawled around.

CONFESSIONS OF A MAN INSANE ENOUGH TO LIVE WITH BEASTS

1.

I remember jacking-off in the closet after putting on my mother's high-heels and looking at my legs in the mirror, slowly drawing a cloth up over my legs, higher and higher as if peeking up the legs of a woman, and being interrupted by two friends coming into the house—"I know he's in here somewhere." My self putting on clothes and then one of them opening the closet door and finding me. "You son of a bitch!" I screamed and chased them both out of the house and heard them talking as they walked away: "What's wrong with him? What the hell's wrong with him?"

2.

K. was an ex-showgirl and she used to show me the clippings and photos. She'd almost won a Miss America contest. I met her in an Alvarado St. bar, which is about as close to getting to skid row as you can get. She had put on weight and age but there was still some sign of a figure, some class, but just a hint and little more. We'd both had it. Neither of us worked and how we made it I'll never know. Cigarettes, wine and a landlady who believed our stories about money coming up but none right now. Mostly we had to have wine.

We slept most of the day but when it began to get dark we had to get up, we felt like getting up:

K: "Shit, I c'd stand a drink."

I'd still be on the bed smoking the last cigarette.

Me: "Well, hell, go down to Tony's and get us a couple of ports."
K: "Fifths?"
Me: "Sure, fifths. And no Gallo. And none of that other, that stuff gave me a headache for two weeks. And get two packs of smokes. Any kind."
K: "But there's only 50 cents here!"
Me: "*I* know that! *Cuff* him for the rest; whatsamata, ya *stupid?*"
K: "He says no more—"
Me: *He* says, *he* says—who is this guy? *God? Fast-talk* him. Smile! Wiggle your can at him! Make his pecker rise! Take him in the back room if necessary, only get that WINE!"
K: "All right, all right."
Me: "And don't come back without it."
K. said she loved me. She used to tie ribbons around my cock and then make a little paper hat for the head.
If she came back without the wine or with only one bottle, then I'd go down like a madman and snarl and bitch and threaten the old man until he gave me what I wanted, and more. Sometimes I'd come back with sardines, bread, chips. It was a particularly good period and when Tony sold the business we started on the new owner who was harder to beard but who could be had. It brought out the best in us.

3.

It was like a wood drill, it might have been a wood drill, I could smell the oil burning, and they'd stick that thing into my head into my flesh and it would drill and bring up blood and puss, and I'd sit there the monkey of my soul-string dangling over the edge of a cliff. I was covered with boils the size of small apples. It was ridiculous and unbelievable. Worst case I ever saw, said one of the docs, and he was old. They'd gather around me like some freak. I was a freak. I'm still a freak. I rode the streetcar back and forth to the charity ward. Children on streetcars would stare and ask their mothers, "What's wrong with that man? Mother, what's wrong with that man's *face*?" And the mother would SHUUSSSHHH!!! That shuussshhh was the worst condemnation, and then they'd continue to let the little bastards and bastardesses stare from over the backs of their seats and I'd look out the window and watch the buildings go by, and I'd be drowning, slugged and drowning, nothing to do. The doctors for lack of anything else called it Acne Vulgaris. I'd sit for hours on a wooden bench while waiting for my wood drill. What a pity story, eh? I remember the old brick buildings, the easy and rested nurses, the doctors laughing, having it made. It was there that I learned of the fallacy of hospitals—that the doctors were kings and the patients were shit and the hospitals were there so the doctors could make it in their starched white superiority, they could make it with the nurses too:—Dr. Dr. Dr. pinch my ass in the elevator, forget the stink of cancer, forget the stink of life. We are not the poor fools, we will never die; we drink our carrot juice, and when we feel bad we can take a pop, a needle, all the dope we need. Cheep, cheep, cheep, life will sing for us, Big-Time us. I'd go in and sit down and they'd put the drill into me. ZIRRRR ZIRRRR ZIRRRR, ZIR, the sun meanwhile raising dahlias and oranges and shining through nurses' dresses driving the poor freaks mad. Zirrrrrr, zirrr, zirr.

"Never saw *anybody* go under the needle like that!"

"Look at him, cold as steel!"

Again a gathering of nurse-fuckers, a gathering of men who owned big homes and had time to laugh and to read and go to plays and buy paintings and forget how to think, forget how to feel anything. White starch and my defeat. The gathering.

"How do you feel?"

"Wonderful."

"Don't you find the needle painful?"

"Fuck you."

"What?"

"I said—fuck you."

"He's just a boy. He's bitter. Can't blame him. How old are you?"

"Fourteen."

"I was only praising you for your courage, the way you took the needle. You're tough."

"Fuck you."

"You can't talk to me that way."

"Fuck you. Fuck you. Fuck you."

"You ought to bear up better. Supposing you were blind?"

"Then I wouldn't have to look at your goddamned face."

"The kid's crazy."

"Sure he is, leave him alone."

That was some hospital and I never realized that 20 years later I'd be back, again in the charity ward. Hospitals and jails and whores: these are the universities of life. I've got several degrees. Call me Mr.

4.

I was shacked with another one. We were on the 2nd floor of a court and I was working. That's what almost killed me, drinking all night and working all day. I kept throwing a bottle through the same window. I used to take that window down to a glass place at the corner and get it fixed, get a pane of glass put in. Once a week I did this. The man looked at me very strangely but he always took my money which looked all right to him. I'd been drinking heavily, steadily for 15 years, and one morning I woke up and there it was: blood streaming out of my mouth and ass. Black turds. Blood, blood, waterfalls of blood. Blood stinks worse than shit. She called a doctor and the ambulance came after me. The attendants said I was too big to carry down the steps and asked me to walk down. "O.k., men," I said. "Glad to oblige—don't want you to work too hard." Outside I got onto the stretcher; they opened it for me and I climbed on like a wilted flower. One hell of a flower. The neighbors had their heads out the windows, they stood on their steps as I went by. They saw me drunk most of the time. "Look, Mabel," one of them said, "there goes that horrible man!" "God have mercy on his soul!" the answer came. Good old Mabel. I let go a mouthful of red over the edge of the stretcher and somebody went OOOOOhhhhhhooooh.

Even though I was working I didn't have any money so it was back to the charity ward. The ambulance was packed. They had shelves in the ambulance and everybody was everywhere. "Full house," said the driver, "let's go." It was a bad ride. We swayed, we tilted. I made every effort to hold the blood in as I didn't want to get anybody stinking. "Oh," I heard a Negro woman's voice, "I can't believe this is happening to me, I can't believe it, oh God help me!"

God gets pretty popular in places like that.

They put me in a dark basement and somebody gave me something in a glass of water and that was that. Every now and then

I would vomit some blood into the bedpan. There were four or five of us down there. One of the men was drunk—and insane—but he seemed strong. He got off his cot and wandered around, stumbled around, falling across the other men, knocking things over, "Wa wa was, I am wawa the joba, I am juba I am jumma jubba wasta, I am juba." I grabbed the water pitcher to hit him with but he never came near me. He finally fell down in a corner and passed out. I was in the basement all night and until noon the next day. Then they moved me upstairs. The ward was overloaded. They put me in a dark corner. "Ooh, he's gonna die in that dark corner," one of the nurses said. "Yeah," said the other one.

I got up one night and couldn't make it to the can. I heaved blood all over the middle of the floor. I fell down and was too weak to get up. I called for a nurse but the doors to the ward were covered with tin and three to six inches thick and they couldn't hear. A nurse came by about once every two hours to check for corpses. They rolled a lot of dead out at night. I couldn't sleep and used to watch them. Slip a guy off the bed and pull him onto the roller and pull the sheet over his head. Those rollers were well-oiled. I hollered, "Nurse!" not knowing especially why. "Shut up!" one of the old men told me, "we want to sleep." I passed out.

When I came to all the lights were on. Two nurses were trying to pick me up. "I told you not to get out of bed," one of them said. I couldn't talk. Drums were in my head. I felt hollowed out. It seemed as if I could hear everything, but I couldn't see, only flares of light, it seemed. But no panic, fear; only a sense of waiting, waiting for anything and not caring.

"You're too big," one of them said, "get in this chair."

They put me in the chair and slid me along the floor. I didn't feel like more than six pounds.

Then they were around me: people. I remember a doctor in a green gown, an operating gown. He seemed angry. He was talking to the head nurse.

"Why hasn't this man had a transfusion? He's down to . . . c.c.'s."

"His papers passed through downstairs while I was upstairs and then they were filed before I saw them. And, besides Doctor, he doesn't have any blood credit."

"I want some blood up here and I want it up here NOW!"

"Who the hell is this guy," I thought, "very odd. Very strange for a doctor."

They started the transfusions—nine pints of blood and eight of glucose.

A nurse tried to feed me roast beef with potatoes and peas and carrots for my first meal. She put the tray before me.

"Hell, I can't eat this," I told her, "this would kill me!"

"Eat it," she said, "it's on your list, it's on your diet."

"Bring me some milk," I said.

"You eat that," she said, and walked away.

I left it there.

Five minutes later she came running into the ward.

"Don't EAT THAT!" she screamed, "you can't HAVE THAT!! There's been a mistake on the list!"

She carried it away and came back with a glass of milk.

As soon as the first bottle of blood emptied into me they sat me up on a roller and took me down to the x-ray room. The doctor told me to stand up. I kept falling over backwards.

"GOD DAMN IT," he screamed, "YOU MADE ME RUIN ANOTHER FILM! NOW STAND THERE AND DON'T FALL DOWN!"

I tried but I couldn't stand up. I fell over backwards.

"Oh shit," he said to the nurse, "take him away."

Easter Sunday the Salvation Army band played right under our window at 5 a.m. They played horrible religious music, played it badly and loudly, and it swamped me, ran through me, almost murdered me. I felt as close to death that morning as I have ever felt. It was an inch away, a hair away. Finally they left for another part of the grounds and I began to climb back toward life. I would say that that morning they probably killed a half dozen captives with their music.

Then my father showed with my whore. She was drunk and I knew he had given her money for drink and deliberately brought her before me drunk in order to make me unhappy. The old man and I were enemies of long standing—everything I believed in he disbelieved and the other way around. She swayed over my bed, red-faced and drunk.

"Why did you bring her like that?" I asked. "Why didn't you wait until another day?"

"I told you she was no good! I always told you she was no good!"

"You got her drunk and then brought her here. Why do you keep knifing me?"

"I told you she was no good, I told you, I *told* you!"

"You son of a bitch, one more word out of you and I'm going to take this needle out of my arm and get up and whip the shit out of you!"

He took her by the arm and they left.

I guess they had phoned them that I was going to die. I was continuing to hemorrhage. That night the priest came.

"Father," I said, "no offense, but please, I'd like to die without any rites, without any words."

I was surprised then because he swayed and rocked in disbelief; it was almost as if I had hit him. I say I was surprised because I thought those boys had more cool than that. But then, they wipe their asses too.

"Father, talk to me," an old man said, "you can talk to me."

The priest went over to the old man and everybody was happy.

Thirteen days from the night I entered I was driving a truck and lifting packages weighing up to 50 pounds. A week later I had my first drink—the one they said would kill me.

I guess someday I'll die in that goddamned charity ward. I just can't seem to get away.

5.

My luck was down again and I was too nervous at this time from excessive wine-drinking; wild-eyed, weak; too depressed to find my usual stop-gap, rest-up job as shipping clerk or stock boy, so I went down to the meat packing plant and walked into the office.

"Haven't I seen you before?" the man asked.

"No," I lied.

I'd been there two or three years before, gone through all the paper work, the medical and so forth, and they led me down steps four floors down and it had gotten colder and colder and the floors had been covered with a sheen of blood, green floors, green walls. He had explained the job to me—which was to push a button and then from this hole in the wall there came a noise like the crushing of fullbacks or elephants falling, and here it came—something dead, a lot of it, bloody, and he showed me, you take it and throw it on the truck and push the button and another one comes along. Then he walked away. When he did I took off my smock, my tin hat, my boots (issued three sizes too small) and walked up the stairway and out of there. Now I was back.

"You look a little old for the job."

"I want to toughen up. I need hard work, good hard work," I lied.

"Can you handle it?"

"I'm nothing but guts. I used to be in the ring, I've fought the best."

"Oh, yes?"

"Yeah."

"Umm, I can see by your face. You must have been in some fierce ones."

"Never mind my face. I had fast hands. Still have. I had to take some dives, had to make it look good."

"I follow boxing. I don't recall your name."

"I fought under another name, Kid Stardust."

"Kid Stardust? I don't recall a Kid Stardust."

"I fought in South America, Africa, Europe, the islands, I fought in the tank towns. That's why there're all these gaps in my employment record—I don't like to put down boxer because people think I am kidding or lying. I just leave the blanks and to hell with it."

"All right, show up for your med. at 9:30 a.m. tomorrow and we'll put you to work. You say you want hard work?"

"Well, if you have something else . . ."

"No, not right now. You know, you look close to 50 years old. I wonder if I'm doing the right thing? We don't like you people to waste our time."

"I'm not people—I'm Kid Stardust."

"O.k., kid," he laughed, "we'll put you to WORK!"

I didn't like the way he said it.

Two days later I walked through the passgate into the wooden shack where I showed an old man my slip with my name on it: Henry Chinaski and he sent me on to the loading dock—I was to see Thurman. I walked on over. There were a row of men sitting on a wooden bench and they looked at me as if I were a homosexual or a basket case.

I looked at them with what I imagined to be easy disdain and drawled in my best backalley fashion:

"Where's Thurman. I'm supposed to see th' guy."
Somebody pointed.
"Thurman?"
"Yeah?"
"I'm workin' for ya."
"Yeah?"
"Yeah."
He looked at me.
"Where's yor boots?"
"Boots? Got none," I said.
He reached under the bench and handed me a pair, an old hardened stiff pair. I put them on. Same old story: three sizes too small. My toes were crushed and bent under.
Then he gave me a bloody smock and a tin helmet. I put them on. I stood there while he lit a cigarette, or as the English might say: while he lighted his cigarette. He threw away the match with a calm and manly flourish.
"Come on."
They were all Negroes and when I walked up they looked at me as if they were Black Muslims. I was over six feet but they were all taller, and if not taller then two or three times as wide.
"Hank!" Thurman hollered.
Hank, I thought. Hank, just like me. That's nice.
I was already sweating under the tin helmet.
"Put 'im to WORK!!"
Jesus christ o jesus christ. What ever happened to the sweet and easy nights? Why doesn't this happen to Walter Winchell who believes in the American Way? Wasn't I one of the most brilliant students in Anthropology? What happened?
Hank took me over and stood me in front of an empty truck a half block long that stood in the dock.
"Wait here."
Then several of the Black Muslims came running up with the wheel-barrows painted a scabby and lumpy white like whitewash mixed in with henshit. And each wheelbarrow was loaded with mounds of hams that floated in thin, watery blood. No, they didn't float in the blood, they sat in it, like lead, like cannonballs, like death.
One of the boys jumped into the truck behind me and the other began throwing the hams at me and I caught them and threw them

to the guy behind me who turned and threw the ham into the back of the truck. The hams came fast FAST and they were heavy and they got heavier. As soon as I threw one ham and turned, another was already on the way to me through the air. I knew that they were trying to break me. I was soon sweating sweating as if faucets had been turned on, and my back ached, my wrists ached, my arms hurt, everything hurt and I was down to the last impossible ounce of limp energy. I could barely see, barely summon myself to catch one more ham and throw it, one more ham and throw it. I was splashed in blood and kept getting the soft dead heavy *flump* in my hands, the ham giving a little like a woman's butt, and I'm too weak to talk and say, "hey, what the HELL'S the matter with you guys?" The hams are coming and I am spinning, nailed like a man on a cross under a tin helmet, and they keep running up barrows full of hams hams hams and at last they are all empty, and I stand there swaying and breathing the yellow electric light. It was night in hell. Well, I always liked night work.

"Come on!"

They took me into another room. Up in the air through a large entrance high in the far wall one half a steer, or it might have been a whole one, yes, they were whole steers, come to think of it, all four legs, and one of them came out of the hole on a hook, having just been murdered, and the steer stopped right over me, it hung right over me there on that hook.

"They've just killed it," I thought, "they've killed the damn thing. How can they tell a man from a steer? How do they know that I am not a steer?"

"ALL RIGHT—SWING IT!"

"Swing it?"

"That's right—DANCE WITH IT!"

"What?"

"O for christ's sake! *George* come here!"

George got under the dead steer. He grabbed it. ONE. He ran forward. TWO. He ran backwards. THREE. He ran far forward. The steer was almost parallel to the ground. Somebody hit a button and he had it. He had it for the meat markets of the world. He had it for the gossiping cranky well-rested stupid housewives of the world at 2 o'clock in the afternoon in their housecoats, dragging at red-stained cigarettes and feeling almost nothing.

They put me under the next steer.

ONE.
TWO.
THREE.

I had it. Its dead bones against my living bones, its dead flesh against my living flesh, and the bone and the weight cut in, I thought of a sexy cunt sitting across from me on a couch with her legs crossed high and me with a drink in my hand, slowly and surely talking my way toward and into the blank mind of her body, and Hank hollered, "HANG HER IN THE TRUCK!"

I ran toward the truck. The shame of defeat taught me in American schoolyards as a boy told me that I must not drop the steer to the ground because this would prove that I was a coward and not a man and that I didn't therefore deserve much, just sneers and laughs, you had to be a winner in America, there wasn't any way out, you had to learn to fight for nothing, don't question, and besides if I dropped the steer I might have to pick it up, and I knew I could never pick it up. Besides it would get dirty. I didn't want it to get dirty, or rather—they didn't want it to get dirty.

I ran it into the truck.

"HANG IT!"

The hook which hung from the roof was dull as a man's thumb without a fingernail. You let the bottom of the steer slide back and went for the top, you poked the top part against the hook again and again but the hook would not go through. *Mother ass*!! It was all gristle and fat, tough, tough.

"COME ON! COME ON!"

I gave it my last reserve and the hook came through, it was a beautiful sight, a miracle, that hook coming through, that steer hanging there by itself completely off my shoulder, hanging for the housecoats and butchershop gossip.

"MOVE ON!"

A 285 pound Negro, insolent, sharp, cool, murderous, walked in, hung his meat with a snap, looked down at me.

"We stays in line here!"

"O.k., ace."

I walked out in front of him. Another steer was waiting for me. Each time I loaded one I was sure that was the last one I could handle but I kept saying

one more
just one more

then I
quit.
Fuck
it.

They were waiting for me to quit, I could see the eyes, the smiles when they thought I wasn't looking. I didn't want to give them victory. I went for another steer. The player. One last lunge of the big-time washed-up player. I went for the meat.

Two hours I went on then somebody hollered, "BREAK."

I had made it. A ten minute rest, some coffee, and they'd never make me quit. I walked out behind them toward a lunch wagon. I could see the steam rising in the night from the coffee; I could see the doughnuts and cigarettes and coffeecakes and sandwiches under the electric lights.

"HEY, YOU!"

It was Hank. Hank like me.

"Yeah, Hank?"

"Before you take your break, get in that truck and move it out and over to stall 18."

It was the truck we had just loaded, the one a half block long. Stall 18 was across the yard.

I managed to open the door and get up inside the cab. It had a soft leather seat and the seat felt so good that I knew if I didn't fight it I would soon be asleep. I wasn't a truck driver. I looked down and saw a half-dozen gear shifts, breaks, pedals and so forth. I turned the key and managed to start the engine. I played with pedals and gear shifts until the truck started to roll and then I drove it across the yard to stall 18, thinking all the while—by the time I get back the lunch wagon will be gone. This was tragedy to me, real tragedy. I parked the truck, cut the engine and sat there a minute feeling the soft goodness of that leather seat. Then I opened the door and got out. I missed the step or whatever was supposed to be there and I fell to the ground in my bloody smock and christ tin helmet like a man shot. It didn't hurt, I didn't feel it. I got up just in time to see the lunch wagon driving off through the gate and down the street. I saw them walking back in toward the dock laughing and lighting cigarettes.

I took off my boots, I took off my smock, I took off my tin helmet and walked to the shack at the yard entrance. I threw the smock, helmet and boots across the counter. The old man looked at me:

"What? You quittin' this GOOD job?"

"Tell 'em to mail me my check for two hours or tell 'em to stick it up their ass, I don't give a damn!"

I walked out. I walked across the street to a Mexican bar and drank a beer and then got a bus to my place. The American schoolyard had beat me again.

6:

The next night I was sitting in a bar between a woman with a rag on her head and a woman without a rag on her head, and it was just another bar—dull, imperfect, desperate, cruel, shitty, poor, and the small men's room reeked to make you heave, and you couldn't crap there, only piss, vomiting, turning your head away, looking for light, praying for the stomach to hold just one more night.

I had been in there about three hours drinking and buying drinks for the one without the rag on her head. She didn't look bad: expensive shoes, good legs and tail; just on the edge of falling apart, but then that's when they look the sexiest—to me.

I bought another drink, two more drinks.

"That's it," I told her, "I'm broke."

"You're kidding."

"No."

"You got a place to stay?"

"Two more days on the rent."

"You working?"

"No."

"What do you do?"

"Nothing."

"I mean, how have you made it?"

"I was a jockey's agent for a while. Had a good boy but they caught him carrying a battery into the starting gate twice. They barred him. Did a little boxing, gambling, even tried chicken farming—used to sit up all night guarding them from the wild dogs in the hills, it was tough, and then one day I left a cigar burning in the pen and I burned up half of them plus all my good roosters. I tried panning gold in Northern California, I was a barker at the beach, I tried the market, I tried selling short—nothing worked, I'm a failure."

"Drink up, she said, and come with me."

That "come with me" sounded good. I drank up and followed her out. We walked up the street and stopped in front of a liquor store.

"Now you keep quiet," she said, "let me do the talking."

We went in. She got some salami, eggs, bread, bacon, beer, hot mustard, pickles, two fifths of good whiskey, some Alka Seltzer and some mix. Cigarettes and cigars.

"Charge it to Willie Hansen," she told the clerk.

We walked outside with the stuff and she called a cab from the box at the corner. The cab showed and we climbed in back.

"Who's Willie Hansen?" I asked.

"Never mind," she said.

Up at my place she helped me put the perishables in the refrigerator. Then she sat down on the couch and crossed those good legs and sat there kicking and twisting an ankle, looking down at her shoe, that spiked and beautiful shoe. I peeled the top off a fifth and stood there mixing two strong drinks. I was king again.

That night in bed I stopped in the middle of it and looked down at her.

"What's your name?" I asked.

"What the hell difference does it make?"

I laughed and went on ahead.

The rent ran out and I put everything, which wasn't much, into my paper suitcase, and 30 minutes later we walked back around a wholesale fur shop, down a broken walk, and there was an old two story house.

Pepper (that was her name, she finally gave me her name) rang the bell and told me—

"You stand back, just let him see me, and when the buzzer sounds I'll push the door open and you follow me in."

Willie Hansen always peeked down the stairway to the halfway point where he had a mirror that showed him who was at the door and then he made up his mind whether to be home or not.

He decided to be home. The buzzer rang and I followed Pepper on in, leaving my suitcase at the bottom of the steps.

"Baby!" he met her at the top of the steps, "so *good* to see you!"

He was pretty old and only had one arm. He put the arm around her and kissed her.

Then he saw me.

"Who's this guy?"

"O, Willie, I want you to meet a friend of mine. This is The Kid."

"Hi!" I said.

He didn't answer me.

"The Kid? He don't look like a kid."

"Kid Lanny, he used to fight under the name Kid Lanny."

"Kid Lancelot," I said.

We went on up into the kitchen and Willie took out a bottle and poured some drinks. We sat at the table.

"How do you like the curtains?" he asked me. "The girls made these curtains for me. The girls have a lot of talent."

"I like the curtains," I told him.

"My arm's getting stiff, I can hardly move my fingers, I think I'm going to die, the doctors can't figure what's wrong. The girls think I'm kidding, the girls laugh at me."

"I believe you," I told him.

We had a couple of more drinks.

"I like you," said Willie, "you look like you been around, you look like you've got class. Most people don't have class. You've got class."

"I don't know anything about class," I said, "but I've been around."

We had some more drinks and went into the front room. Willie put on a sailing cap and sat down at an organ and he began playing the organ with his one arm. It was a very loud organ.

There were quarters and dimes and halves and nickles and pennies all over the floor. I didn't ask questions. We sat there drinking and listening to the organ. I applauded lightly when he finished.

"All the girls were up here the other night," he told me, "and then somebody hollered, RAID! and you should have seen them running, some of them naked and some of them in panties and bras, they all ran out and hid in the garage. It was funny as hell! I sat up here and they came drifting back one by one from the garage. It was sure *funny*!"

"Who was the one who hollered RAID?" I asked.

"I was," he said.

Then he walked into his bedroom and took off his clothes and got into his bed. Pepper walked in and kissed him and talked to him as I walked around picking the coins up off the floor.

When she came out she motioned to the bottom of the stairway. I went down for the suitcase and brought it up.

7.

Everytime he put on that sailor's cap, that captain's cap, in the morning we knew we were going out on the yacht. He'd stand in front of the mirror adjusting it for proper angle and one of the girls would come running in to tell us:

"We're going out on the yacht—Willie's putting on his cap!"

Like the first time. He came out with the cap on and we followed him down to the garage, not a word spoken.

He had an old car, so old it had a rumble seat.

The two or three girls got in front with Willie, sitting on laps, however they made it, they made it, and Pepper and I got in the rumble seat, and she said—"He only goes out when he doesn't have a hangover, and when he's not drinking. The bastard doesn't want anybody else to drink either, so watch it!"

"Hell, I need a drink."

"We all need a drink," she said. She took a pint from her purse and unscrewed the cap. She handed the bottle to me.

"Now wait until he checks us in the rearview mirror. Then the minute his eyes go back on the road take a slug."

I tried it. It worked. Then it was Pepper's turn. By the time we reached San Pedro the bottle was empty. Pepper took out some gum and I lit a cigar and we climbed out.

It was a fine looking yacht. It had two engines and Willie stood there showing me how to start the auxiliary motor in case anything went wrong. I stood there not listening, nodding. Some kind of crap about pulling a rope in order to start the thing.

He showed me how to pull anchor, unmoor from dock, but I was only thinking about another drink, and then we pulled out, and he stood there in the cabin with his captain's cap on steering the thing, and all the girls got around him.

"O, Willie, let me steer!"

"Willie, let me steer!"

I didn't want to steer. He named the boat after himself: THE WILLHAN. Terrible name. He should have called it THE FLOAT-

ING PUSSY.

I followed Pepper down to the cabin and we found more to drink, plenty to drink. We stayed down there drinking. I heard him cut the engine and he came down the steps.

"We're going back in," he said.

"What for?"

"Connie's gone into one of her moods. I'm afraid she'll jump overboard. She won't speak to me. She just sits there staring. She can't swim. I'm afraid she'll jump over."

(Connie was the one with the rag around her head.)

"Let her jump. I'll go get her out. I'll knock her out, I've still got my punch and then I'll pull her in. Don't worry about her."

"No, we're going in. Besides, you people have been *drinking*!"

He went upstairs. I poured some more drinks and lit a cigar.

8.

When we hit dock Willie came down and said he'd be right back. He wasn't right back. He wasn't back for three days and three nights. He left all the girls there. He just drove off in his car.

"He's mad," said one of the girls.

"Yeah," said another.

There was plenty of food and liquor there though, so we stayed and waited for Willie. There were four girls there including Pepper. It was cold down there no matter how much you drank, no matter how many blankets you got under. There was only one way to get warm. The girls made a joke of it—

"I'm NEXT!" one of them would holler.

"I think I'm outa come," another would say.

"You think YOU'RE outa come," I said, "how about ME?"

They laughed. Finally I just couldn't make it anymore.

I found I had my green dice on me and we got down on the floor and started a crap game. Everybody was drunk and the girls had all the money, I didn't have any money, but soon I had quite a bit of money. They didn't quite understand the game and I explained it to them as we went along and I changed the game as we went along to suit the circumstances.

That's how Willie found us when he got back—shooting craps and drunk.

"I DON'T ALLOW GAMBLING ON THIS SHIP!" he screamed from the top of the steps.

Connie climbed up the steps, put her arms around him and stuck her long tongue into his mouth, then grabbed his parts. He came down the steps smiling, poured a drink, poured drinks for us all and we sat there talking and laughing, and he talked about an opera he was writing for the organ, *The Emperor of San Francisco.* I promised him I'd write the words to the music and that night we drove back into town everybody drinking and feeling good. That first trip was almost a carbon of every trip. One night he died and we were all out in the street again, the girls and myself. Some sister back east got every dime and I went to work in a dog biscuit factory.

9.

I'm living in someplace on Kingsley Street and working as a shipping clerk for a place that sold overhead light fixtures.

It was a fairly calm time. I drank a lot of beer each night, often forgetting to eat. I bought a typewriter, an old second-hand Underwood with keys that stuck. I hadn't written anything for ten years. I got drunk on beer and began writing poetry. Pretty soon I had quite a backlog and didn't know what to do with it. I put the whole works into one envelope and mailed it to some new magazine in a small town in Texas. I figured that nobody would take the stuff but at least somebody might get mad, so it wouldn't be wasted entirely.

I got a letter back, I got two letters back, long letters. They said I was a genius, they said I was startling, they said I was God. I read the letters over and over and got drunk and wrote a long letter back. I sent more poems. I wrote poems and letters every night, I was full of bullshit.

The editoress, who was also a writer of sorts, began sending back photos of herself and she didn't look bad, not bad at all. The letters began getting personal. She said nobody would marry her. Her assistant editor, a young male, said he would marry her for half her inheritance but she said she didn't have any money, people only thought she had money. The assistant editor later did a stretch in a mental ward. "Nobody will marry me," she kept writing, "your poems will be featured in our next edition, an all-Chinaski edition, and nobody will ever marry me, nobody, you see I have a deformity, it's my neck, I was born this way. I'll never be married."

I was very drunk one night. "Forget it," I wrote, "I will marry you. Forget about the neck. I am not so hot either. You with your neck and me with my lion-clawed face—I can see us walking down the street together!"

I mailed the thing and forgot all about it, drank another can of beer and went to sleep.

The return mail brought a letter: "Oh, I'm so happy! Everybody looks at me and they say, 'Niki, what happened to you? You're RADIANT, bursting!!! What is it?' I won't tell them! Oh, Henry, I'M SO HAPPY!"

She enclosed some photos, particularly ugly photos. I got scared. I went out and got a fifth of whiskey. I looked at the photos, I drank the whiskey. I got down on the rug:

"O Lord or Jesus what have I done? What have I done? Well, I'll tell you what, Boys, I'm going to devote the rest of my life to making this poor woman happy! It will be hell but I am tough, and what's a better way to go than making somebody *else* happy?"

I got up from the rug, not too sure about the last part. . . .

A week later I was waiting in the bus station, I was drunk and waiting for the arrival of a bus from Texas.

They called the bus over the loudspeaker and I got ready to die. I watched them coming through the doorway trying to match them up with the photographs. And then I saw a young blonde, 23, good legs, live walk, and an innocent and rather snobbish face, pert I'd guess you'd call her, and the neck was not bad at all. I was 35 then.

I walked up to her.

"Are you Niki?"

"Yes."

"I'm Chinaski. Let me have your suitcase."

We walked out to the parking lot.

"I've been waiting for three hours, nervous, jumpy, going through hell waiting. All I could do was to have some drinks in the bar."

She put her hand on the hood of the car.

"This engine's still hot. You bastard you just got here!"

I laughed.

"You're right."

We got into the old car and made it on in. Soon we were married in Vegas, and it took what money I had for that and the bus fare back to Texas.

I got on the bus with her and I had thirty-five cents left in my pocket.

"I don't know if Poppa's gonna like what I did," she said.

"O Jesus o God," I prayed, "help me be strong, help me be brave!"

She necked and squirmed and twisted all the way to that small Texas town. We arrived at 2:30 a.m. and as we got off the bus I thought I heard the bus driver say—"Who's that bum you got there with you, Niki?"

We stood in the street and I said, "What did that busdriver say? What'd he say to you?" I asked, rattling my thirty-five cents in my pocket.

"He didn't say anything. Come on with me."

She walked up the steps of a downtown building.

"Hey, where the hell you going?"

She put a key in the door and the door opened. I looked above the door and carved in the stone were the words: CITY HALL.

We went on in.

"I want to see if I received any mail."

She went into her office and looked through a desk.

"Damn it, no mail!! I'll bet that *bitch* stole my mail!"

"What bitch? What bitch, baby?"

"I have an enemy. Look, follow me."

We went down the hall and she stopped in front of a doorway. She gave me a hairpin.

"Here, see if you can pick this lock."

I stood there trying. I saw the headlines:

FAMED WRITER AND REFORMED PROSTITUTE FOUND BREAKING INTO MAYOR'S OFFICE!

I couldn't pick the lock.

We walked on down to her place, leaped into bed and went at what we had been working toward on the bus.

I'd been there a couple of days when the doorbell rang about 9 a.m. one morning. We were in bed.

"What the hell?" I asked.

"Go get the bell," she said.

I climbed into some clothes and went to the door. A midget was standing there, and every once in a while he shook all over, he had some type of malady. He had on a little chauffeur's cap.

"Mr. Chinaski?"

"Yeah?"

"Mr. Dyer asked me to show you the lands."

"Wait a minute."

I went back on in. "Baby, there's a midget out there and he says a Mr. Dyer wants to show me the lands. He's a midget and he shakes all over.

"Well, go *with* him. That's my father."

"Who, the midget?"

"No, Mr. Dyer."

I put on my shoes and stockings and went out on the porch.

"O.k., buddy," I said, "let's go."

We drove all over town and out of town.

"Mr. Dyer owns that," the midget would point, and I'd look, "and Mr. Dyer owns that," and I'd look.

I didn't say anything.

"All those farms," he said, "Mr. Dyer owns all those farms and he lets them work the land and they split it down the middle."

The midget drove to a green forest. He pointed.

"See the lake?"

"Yeah."

"There's seven lakes in there full of fish. See the turkey walking around?"

"Yeah."

"That's wild turkey. Mr. Dyer rents all that out to a fish and game club which runs it. Of course, Mr. Dyer and any of his friends can go anytime they want. Do you fish or shoot?"

"I've done a lot of shooting in my time," I told him.

We drove on.

"Mr. Dyer went to school there."

"Oh, yeah?"

"Yup, right in that brick building. Now he's bought it and restored it as a kind of monument."

"Amazing."

We drove back in.

"Thanks," I told him.

"Do you want me to come back tomorrow morning? There's more to see."

"No, thanks, it's all right."

I walked back in. I was king again. . .

And it's good to end it right there instead of telling you how I lost it, although it's something about a Turk who wore a purple stickpin in his tie and had fine manners and culture. I didn't have a chance. But the Turk wore off too and the last I heard she was in Alaska married to an Eskimo. She sent me a picture of her baby, and she said she was still writing and truly happy. I told her, "Hang tight, baby, it's a crazy world."

And that, as they say, was that.

CHARLES BUKOWSKI is one of America's best-known contemporary writers of poetry and prose, and, many would claim, its most influential and imitated poet. He was born in Andernach, Germany, to an American soldier father and a German mother in 1920, and brought to the United States at the age of three. He was raised in Los Angeles and lived there for fifty years. He published his first story in 1944 when he was twenty-four and began writing poetry at the age of thirty-five. He died in San Pedro, California, on March 9, 1994, at the age of seventy-three, shortly after completing his last novel, *Pulp* (1994).

During his lifetime he published more than forty-five books of poetry and prose, including the novels *Post Office* (1971), *Factotum* (1975), *Women* (1978), *Ham on Rye* (1982), and *Hollywood* (1989). Among his most recent books are the posthumous editions of *What Matters Most Is How Well You Walk Through the Fire* (1999), *Open All Night: New Poems* (2000), *Beerspit Night and Cursing: The Correspondence of Charles Bukowski and Sheri Martinelli, 1960–1967* (2001), and *Night Torn Mad with Footsteps: New Poems* (2001).

All of his books have now been published in translation in more than a dozen languages and his worldwide popularity remains undiminished. In the years to come Ecco will publish additional volumes of previously uncollected poetry and letters.

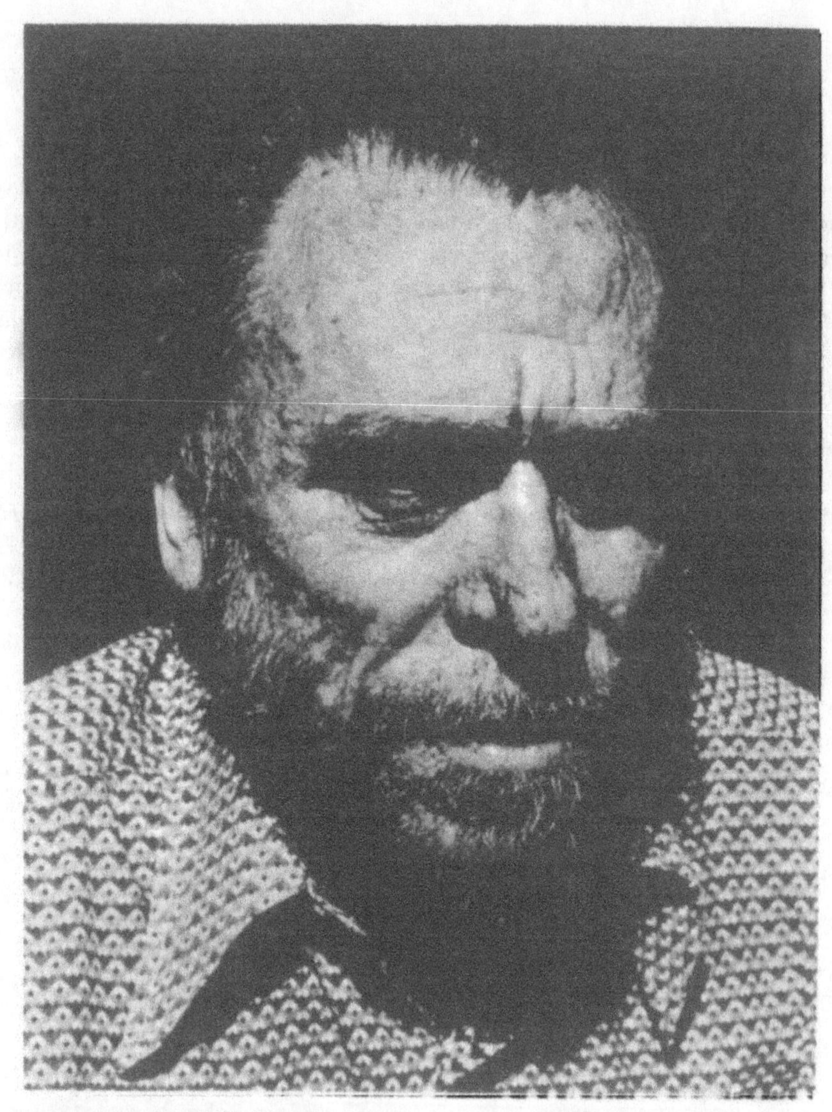

PHOTO: Richard Robinson

ecco
An Imprint of HarperCollins*Publishers*
www.harpercollins.com

ISBN 0-87685-189-8
51500>
EAN
9 780876 851890
USA $15.00 Canada $23.00
0203

www.ingramcontent.com/pod-product-compliance
Lightning Source LLC
LaVergne TN
LVHW030952240325
806630LV00014B/166

* 9 7 8 0 8 7 6 8 5 1 8 9 0 *